I0778938

UPHEAVAL

CC ROBINSON

Book Cover by 100 Covers, Rebecca Yelland.
Interior by Amie McCracken

www.ccrobinsonauthor.com

ISBN Paperback: 978-1962912020
ISBN Ebook: 978-1962912006

Dedicated to Steve

Chapter 1: Julianna

Juli closed the curtains on the darkest night of her life. The lights had gone out a full half hour ago and nothing electronic would power on, not even her cell phone or her precious Prius.

An EMP had struck Cincinnati.

She looked around her sparse living room. Moses hadn't arrived yet. He should have. Had he gotten stuck somewhere en route to her apartment? She ran her fingers through her hair. Had his old beater died after the EMP? Moses claimed his Accord could run through the next apocalypse. But was that true?

She'd have to do this on her own and trust him to find her along the way.

Juli grabbed her ball cap from the scratched wooden coffee table and tucked in her wild curls before heading into her bathroom, her hands resting on the slight swell of her belly. She sat on the tub's edge and dipped the canteens below the water's surface. When the first nuclear bombs had fallen on the east coast, she'd filled her bathtub to the sounds of local network affiliate reporters freaking out, their DC and New York counterparts incinerated in the blasts. This was now her only clean, potable water source and yet, she had to leave it.

She slipped the heavy canteens into her backpack and laced up her favorite black running shoes. Juli checked the full-length mirror, making sure nothing glittered or shone on her, then scribbled a note for Moses and set it next to the tub.

Before she left, Juli lifted her hood over her cap and shouldered her pack, cinching the straps.

Saying a silent prayer for safety, Juli hiked down the emergency exit stairs into the alleyway behind her apartment building. It was quiet. Too quiet. The night was chilly, but not cold enough to make her breath mist in a telltale cloud. The air carried the hint of moisture, the steel scent of an approaching snowfall.

It took her eyes a precious thirty seconds to adjust before she loped off at an easy jog. She headed toward the old brewery and subway tunnels under Cincinnati, where the group of concerned citizens led by her fiancé Moses were meeting up.

Passing one darkened home after another on deserted backstreets, the steady rhythm of her pounding feet and the occasional barking dog broke the silence. She was thankful Moses had introduced her to physical fitness when they'd started dating nine months ago. She was in great shape, the best of her life. And despite her condition, she felt strong, even after a nearly four-mile brisk jog.

Muted voices filtered toward her, and Juli's fingers edged closer to her hip holster and her Beretta. She ducked behind the corner of a building, allowing the shadows cast by the bright moonlight to swallow her. She was so close to her destination. And she'd finally encountered other people. Friend or foe, she couldn't know.

She froze as kids on bikes whizzed by her position, yelling curses and taunts back and forth. They were clearly unconcerned about being caught out after curfew, which had been in place for months. It had all started after race riots rocked Cincinnati following yet another death of a young Black man at the hands of a white police officer. Of course, that was one of many tit-for-tat attacks. Too many. The older white man walking his dog who was attacked by the mob of young Black men. Or the Hispanic woman who died at the hands of an angry white mob. The Black woman who had killed a Hispanic man trying to rob her, who then was attacked by a Hispanic gang, strung up in a tree for the world to see. The names of those who'd died over the years were forgotten in the wake of the nuclear attacks, but the images lingered. The death. The anger.

Who were these kids? As a math teacher at a nearby high school, Juli knew many of the neighborhood youth.

She doubted they were taking a joy ride at three a.m.

Could they be members of one of the new mega-gangs? The mega-gangs sprung up overnight, forming when many single ethnicity gangs linked forces. Moses said they were everywhere, in every city, and had even overtaken a few.

The teens dismounted, huddling in murmured conversation.

As she ducked into the shadows, she remembered the day after the first nuclear attacks. The bombs had incinerated DC, New York, LA and Atlanta, along with the rest of both coasts. She had gone into school as usual, fully expecting students to be reeling and needing comfort. Perhaps counselors would be on site like what happened after a school shooting or national tragedy. Juli could've used an hour with a counselor herself, her mind numb with the shock of the attacks.

What she'd found awoke her to the situation's gravity.

Students were looting Cincinnati's premier magnet high school, while teachers cleaned out their classrooms and hurried away. The principal and the resource officer had blocked the main entrance, searching bags for stolen items. Not that it helped, as students had broken down other exits and had even thrown desks through ground-floor windows to climb out.

Juli had grabbed a few essentials, then snuck out with another teacher after dodging fist fights and a mob looting the vending machines. She'd never forget the two girls fighting over the last Twix bar — all the hair-pulling, nails flying off, and clothes being ripped had astonished her. Honestly, Juli loved chocolate like anyone else, but why fight over it?

The world had sunk into a deep evil. How much worse would it get? No power. No video games. No refrigerators. No light. No shipments of drugs for the gangs to sell.

The chill wind brought her back to the present. The kids had gathered on a front lawn of a normal home in this typical university neighborhood. They broke apart, approaching homes in pairs, the last boy left outside as sentry.

Before Juli could shout a warning, they kicked doors in and gunshots filled the air.

"Hey!" the lookout shouted in her direction. "Whoever you are, just leave! Leave now and you won't get hurt." He wiped his forehead, staring straight at her.

Juli gulped in a scream and scrambled backward through the narrow walkway between homes, emerging into a deserted back alley. The smell of the dumpster made her gag, but worse was the reality of those gunshots. She couldn't allow herself to get trapped here. She had a life to protect.

She jogged at a moderate pace, cold air pricking her cheeks. She twitched her nose at the scent of rotting trash piled high on the curb, swallowing down the urge to vomit. As she rounded a corner, a darkened train loomed ahead, blocking the intersection and her way forward. She drew her weapon at movement in the train's shadow.

"Announce yourself," Juli said.

"Sergeant Moses Reynolds of the 2/75 A-Co, sir!"

Juli chuckled. Everyone was "sir" to an Army Ranger, including your fiancée. She relaxed and holstered her gun. She wrapped her arms around him, noticing his Honda parked by the dumpster in the alley, the engine silent.

"Keep that out, hermosa," he said. "I don't like the looks of this. I'm surprised the neighborhood gangs aren't already stripping it to the bone."

Juli murmured agreement, turning around in his arms to search the darkness. "How did you know where I'd be?"

He released her, raising an eyebrow at her question. "Knew you'd come this way, eventually. Figured we could head to the bunker together if I could catch up with you." He searched her face. "You made awfully good time."

She shrugged. "I wasn't about to stay for whatever chaos my next-door neighbor would start." Juli was positive he was a leader of one of the new mega-gangs. He had moved in a week before the nuclear attacks, meeting at night with rough-looking men. The comings and goings of that apartment caused Juli to call the police. Their hands were tied, they said, unless she saw illegal activity. Though she'd noticed the plainclothes officers walking her street since then.

As they headed southward inside the railroad track fence and approached the engine, they heard shouts and loud thuds behind them. Moses tugged Juli toward the shadows closer to the fence as dark forms materialized on the other side. She sensed his readiness next to her.

"Well, look who's out for a midnight stroll!"

Moses pushed her behind him and gestured for her to climb up the gravel incline and across the connector between the front two engines. He scrambled after her as the men leaped the fence and pursued them. Juli tucked behind the last engine's corner, while Moses took up position across the connector, his Beretta aimed at the man's chest.

"Halt where you are! Sergeant Reynolds of the 2nd Ranger Battalion here and I am prepared to defend my group. Stand down and walk away!"

Peels of mocking laughter erupted from the other side of the train right before bullets strafed his position. Moses ducked behind the steel car.

"Identify yourselves! Drop your weapons and back away from the train. Hands where I can see them! That's an order!"

Gunfire pinging off the metal engine was their reply.

Moses locked gazes with Juli, her Beretta at the ready, her finger on the trigger. He switched to his M4 rifle, by far a superior weapon.

Moses mouthed, "Hunting — on three," before they burst together into the space between the engines. Working seamlessly as if they'd done this their entire lives, they took out the combatants across the connector. Gunfire erupted above them, and Juli fired at the person on the train car's roof while Moses ducked and shot another fighter crawling underneath the engine. A dull thud and gravel sprays behind them made her spin. She'd scored a hit.

A thin man tumbled to the ground as a glassy stare met her own, her bullet embedded in his forehead. Juli's pulse raced. Surely Moses had seen death in his Ranger tours, but this was Juli's first kill.

A gunshot whizzed by her shoulder, and she dove.

"Your six!" Moses yelled from the ladder of the second engine car.

Juli fired shot after shot into the night, cursing quietly when she missed and barking a "Ramirez down" and "Ramirez up" to signal reloading. Reflection on the death and destruction her gun wrought would come later. Much later.

When the last fighter fell to Moses's bullet, clutching his chest, Juli surveyed the scene.

Death surrounded them. Only Moses and Juli were standing.

She wiped blood from her temple. His eyes went wide as he raced to her side.

"You're shot!"

Juli nodded. "Grazed. It smarts like anything. Do you have your field kit?"

She couldn't focus on the dead man at her feet. Nor the injured fighter struggling to breathe his last. She walked away from the engine, not caring where she went. She had to get away.

Away from the reality of death.

"Of course."

The terseness in his voice snapped her eyes to his face. A muscle ticked in his jaw, the only sign of Moses's anger. Juli forced a deep breath into her lungs and walked toward his car, the bunker and safety.

Moses silently dug out an antiseptic swab and dabbed her wound, a hand on her shoulder steadying her, grounding her to reality.

"Doesn't need stitches. An inch to the left and you'd be dead. Those were gang bangers. But the way they attacked…"

Moses trailed his hand down her arm.

Was all this coordinated? A part of a bigger plan? The drug wars adding to the race riots meant to create chaos that, when combined with a nuclear attack and an EMP, would bring the mighty US of A to its knees?

Moses hadn't told her everything. But she'd put two and two together. His training local police departments in Ranger Unconventional Warfare methods and the gangs aligned with specific ethnic groups were clear warning signs.

"We need to move." Moses led them back toward his car, his eyes scanning their surroundings.

"Who do you think they were?" Juli asked, passing a dead man.

"Doesn't matter." Moses eyed the bi-racial man and another Latino folded in a heap atop an expanding blood pool. "They're the enemy. And they were trying to kill us. Rules of engagement, my ass. Next time I'm not wasting precious seconds telling them who I am and to stand down."

Juli jogged beside him, her mind on everything that just happened.

She saw the entire scene as if she floated above, an angel of death surveying her work. She'd killed people tonight. Juli wanted to curl up in a ball and cry her eyes out, praying for forgiveness and for their souls. Yet, if she stopped now, she could be next. Juli shoved her horror and remorse deep down for another day.

"My car's over here."

They climbed into his ancient Honda Accord. The hum of the machine made Juli want to cry in relief. She would never take little things for granted again. After her Prius failed to start, she wondered if any cars would run. Guess her all-electric vehicle was more the exception than the rule. How they'd refuel the Accord was another matter entirely.

"How was the training?" Juli needed to talk about something normal. Routine. She knew that for what it was. A trauma stress reaction. But she didn't care.

Moses sighed and eyed her. "Alright, I guess. Don't know what to do now, though. This is bigger than anyone thought. Part of me just wants to get you to Canada and safety, if we can, then come back to salvage what's left of the Army."

"Moses, we can't abandon everyone. We said we'd do this together."

Moses and Juli had joined with other concerned citizens before they'd started dating, building relationships as they watched their nation crumble around them. Not even two weeks ago, they'd met in the tunnels, pondering the race riots and what they could do to stop them. Then the bombs had fallen on the coasts, prompting another emergency meeting, which Moses had missed while he was in Indiana training local PD's. Cincinnati wasn't the only city at war.

"Command is in chaos still." Moses interrupted her thoughts. "The few higher-ups left alive are saying incredible things. That China, Iran and North Korea collaborated on the nuclear attacks. We didn't know Iran could launch ballistic missiles, but before they took the sat defense system out, other nations, I can't say who, saw incomings from those three countries. Of course, we were all too late. The attackers coordinated their strikes by taking out our defenses first. How the shits found those, I have no clue. Inside job, is my guess. But now? Are foreign troops coming? Is that what we have to contend with? Or maybe more of these mega-gangs? How big will those get? It's hard to not feel like we're fighting a losing battle. I want you out of here."

Juli clenched her teeth. Didn't he understand she wasn't willing to be away from him? He must be insane to think she'd be ok with that.

Chapter 2: Moses

They pulled into the dark parking lot near the now-silent Music Hall, slowing to weave their way underground.

After Moses parked and they had swung their heavy packs onto their backs, he led the way back to the surface, to the access point for the tunnel system in a mixed-use warehouse. A company which led tours into the tunnels operated in the front half, their staff joking about the tunnels' ghosts or regaling guests with the tales of old brewers rolling the barrels from brewery to custom house. That business, like so many others, was a thing of the past. Who had time for ghost stories when life had become a living horror film?

One of their group rented an office in the warehouse. Isley had discovered the tunnel entrance by accident while searching for cleaning equipment. The concealed panel inside a closet led into a massive underground complex, empty for decades since prohibition's end. It was the perfect place to gather and strategize.

To the light of Juli's flashlight, Moses unlocked the closet door, releasing cool air into the room. He gestured for her to go ahead of him down the steep stairs, closing and locking the door behind them.

They hurried through the rough-hewn tunnels, wooden boards intermittently reinforced with steel supports holding back the earth. Moses noted fresh footprints on the dusty ground. They weren't the first to arrive.

Moses pushed aside the disguised panel, caked on the outside with dirt, and dialed the passcode on the old-school safe lock. The door popped open. As he descended the short staircase and entered the concrete tunnels, Juli replaced the panel and closed the airlock behind them. He grabbed her hand, leading as they made their way to their meeting place, in what had been a dance hall in a speakeasy. Moses would've loved to witness those days but was thankful the speakeasy's existence was now lost to time.

Moses rapped the coded knock before using yet another key to open the door. A gun barrel greeted them before a smiling Matthew Chen holstered his weapon and briskly hugged them both.

"Thank God, you made it, Moses," Matthew said over his shoulder, his flashlight's beam bouncing ahead of him. "Reverend Thompson's here. We've been waiting for you all."

"I was in Dayton. Had to get back, then find Juli." He squeezed Juli's hand. He was proud of her for following his evacuation instructions, even though he knew she'd had to swallow her terror. "When did you all arrive?"

"I got here thirty minutes ago. Rev's been in and out for a week. Said he's preparing for whatever's next. Good thing, too. He added to our supplies."

Excellent. Their friend group had squirreled away months' worth of canned goods, non-perishables and water. Plus guns, ammunition and body armor. They were ready for whatever came next. Had been getting more prepared with each passing week, as the chaos in the city had risen.

Footsteps made them both spin. Juli raised her revolver and flicked off the safety.

Moses pressed the gun toward the floor with a chuckle. His fiancé was a badass.

"Friendlies," he said.

"How did you know?"

"Just us!" Isley called out. "Angie's coming, too."

"Let's get settled," Matthew said, greeting his wife, Angie, with a kiss on the cheek as she walked into the room. "We need to make plans. And Moses, I hope you have more information this time."

Moses grunted. "You won't like it, though."

Matthew shrugged and ran a hand through his stiff black hair, making it stand on end. Moses eyed his friend, reading Matthew's nervousness like a book.

Most of them were single, a mix of men and women. Juli had expressed qualms about being the sole female when Moses had invited her. He'd assured her, and, sure enough, she'd fit right in with everyone, especially with Angie. He was thankful their group was a broad mix of races, another surprise given the racial tensions in their city and nation going back twenty-plus years. No, scratch that. A few centuries.

But their love for the nation and concern for its decline had made them take action. Would they stay together, though? Or would they split among those who wanted to flee and those who would fight?

As the others gathered, flashlights cast an eerie glow and ominous shadows around the room. Figures wearing dark clothing sat like boulders in a circle, only their bared faces visible in the dim light. Juli waved to the other women. Moses didn't miss the group's tight smiles. People were more scared than usual. And he agreed. They had good cause to be terrified. Heck, Moses was a little scared, too.

Matthew cleared his throat. "Let's hear from Moses first. What's the situation with the military and police?"

Moses updated the group on the loss of the DOD chain of command after the nuclear attacks and, with the EMPs, the breakdown in communications. The nuclear attacks had decimated most of the stateside Army and Navy, then the EMP rendered the Air Force useless.

And without cell phone communication to coordinate movements, how could the military do anything? Use carrier pigeons? Bike messengers?

America was a sitting duck.

As he spoke, Moses felt hope drain out of the group, like water squeezed from a sponge. He finished his update, and the room dissolved into shouted suggestions.

"We definitely need to fight these gangs."

"How can we? They have bigger firepower than us."

The debate continued, and Moses realized Juli had remained silent. He raised his brows at her, tilting his head toward the group. She leaned in.

"Moses," Juli whispered. "Didn't you say the police are still fighting these mega-gangs? And isn't the National Guard in Cincinnati?"

"Yeah," Moses said as the debate raged around them. He listened to Juli with one ear and everyone else with the other. It seemed most wanted to flee for their lives, despite their bravado before the nuclear attacks.

"Maybe all the police and National Guard need is a few citizens willing to organize neighborhood militia. The authorities can lead, but surely regular citizens can repulse these kids? It's not like they're real military, right? They're just kids in a gang. The two of us took out more than a dozen on our way here tonight. Sure, we're trained, but citizens far outnumber the gang bangers. If we got guns into neighborhood watch hands, activate ordinary people, let them defend their neighborhoods. They'd work with the police. And the Guard can attack the gangs' strongholds."

The room fell silent as Juli spoke.

"You know," Matthew interjected. "She's right. This could work. Ian, don't you have a contact in Metro? And Donna, don't you know the mayor?"

Suddenly, the group tossed ideas around, their voices mingling as excitement grew. Moses watched Juli's smile widen, proud of her for standing her ground and holding her convictions when others had allowed fear to control them.

"Moses, don't you see? We can do this!"

Moses examined her, memorizing her facial features. "You really want to do this?"

"Yes!" Juli shouted as she vaulted to her feet. "I won't run. It's what we planned, but it feels cowardly. I'm not letting these thugs steal my country! We're going to take our streets back, if we have to do it one street at a time! Now, let's get moving! We have people to wake up."

With a loud cry, the others jumped up, pumping fists into the air and heading for the group's armory.

Moses tugged her into a tight hug. "You are such a dynamo. I never would've asked this of you. But if you're in, I'm in. Let's take back Cincinnati."

She pulled his head down and kissed him hard, making him groan. He'd missed her with every fiber of his being. "Moses, let's go wake up the priest and get married tonight. No more playing around. We have a nation to rescue from terrorists and I want to do it as your wife."

"You've got a deal." He buried his face in her hair, cradling her to his chest.

How he loved this woman. Brave, selfless, and the mother of his unborn child.

Chapter 3: Julianna

The skyscrapers of downtown Cincinnati loomed above them, dark in the pre-dawn chill almost two weeks later. Juli tightened the strings of her hoodie around her face and hunched her shoulders, feeling like she had a target in the middle of her back. The gold band on her left ring finger felt natural, as if it'd lived there her entire life.

"Moses."

Her husband grasped her hand, fingering her wedding band. Her husband. That reality would take a while to sink in. But it didn't remove the feeling of being watched.

"I know, I feel it too," he said, his head on swivel.

"I thought they cleared these buildings."

"They did, but who makes sure they stay empty?"

The chains across the glass doors mocked her sense of security. She couldn't shake the touch of eyes following them as they crept through the shadows to the Potter Stewart US Courthouse in downtown Cincinnati. Toward a secret meeting of city, state, and federal leaders. Those who were still alive, at least. Those whose homes the mega-gangs hadn't invaded, targeting anyone with any modicum of power. Their radio had crackled with news of assassinations of township leaders across the city. Then there were the judges, police, and even corporate leaders. They'd lost too many of them to the fighting between the ethnic-centric militias. A twisted version of street justice had permeated the city in recent months, cutting off the head of what used to be a vibrant metropolis and plunging Cincinnati into chaos.

And now this. Mega-gangs roving the city, killing pedestrians on-sight, looting and pillaging seemingly at random.

The acting police chief had pled with Moses to help the remaining leaders organize the city's defense. Juli wondered if it was too little, too late.

Moses halted at the corner of the federal building. "You see them?"

Juli's heart stuttered. Teens in jeans and dark hoodies toting an array of weapons trotted up the wide steps of the courthouse.

"Damn. How did they know?"

"Let's try the back docks," Moses said, tugging her away.

She sprinted to keep up as he circled the block.

"Won't they have thought of this?" she asked.

"I'm hoping not, otherwise we'll lose the rest of our leaders."

"We have a rat somewhere."

"Obviously."

Moses slowed as they approached the courthouse back loading docks, silent as a tomb except for the soft crunch of their footsteps on the loose gravel. Moses drew his Beretta and eased the metal door open. He lifted a finger to his lips.

"Stay behind me."

Juli tucked a stray curl into her ballcap, her Beretta at the ready.

"Do you know where you're going?"

"Not exactly. Let's try the southwest corner for stairs."

The squat courthouse was a northward facing U shape. They ran along the southmost hallway, their shoes squeaking too loudly against the tile. Juli followed Moses into the emergency stairwell, easing the metal door shut behind them as he sprinted up two levels. She kept up, thankful for their training before the world had collapsed.

Moses looked through the block glass window, shaking his head. "Too dark. I can't see a thing." He lifted his backpack off his shoulders and tossed her a pair of goggles, donning his own set.

"Do the gangs have these, too?"

"Some do. But I hope these don't. It'll ruin our advantage. And we're already outnumbered." He turned to her, concern pinching his brows and puckering his mouth. "If I'm shot, I want you to run. Leave me." Moses rested a hand on her belly and placed a gentle kiss on her forehead. "Understand?"

Juli nodded, though she wouldn't do it. He was worried about their unborn child, but she couldn't contemplate life without him.

"Let's get our leaders out."

Moses launched into the hallway, clearing it before motioning her to follow. Juli walked in a crouch behind him as he tested every door until they arrived at the conference room. Moses gave the coded knock, and the door opened.

They removed their night-vision goggles, blinded by a few strategically placed candles.

Juli nodded to the mayor, a stout Black woman in her fifties wearing jeans and a sweatshirt. At least she hadn't dressed in her usual tailored pantsuits and heels. The acting police chief extended a hand to Moses.

"Thank you for coming, sergeant," he said. Juli blanched at seeing the white man in full uniform, his cap tilting jauntily to the side, "Tracy" emblazoned on his chest. She wondered if he had a death wish walking around the city in uniform.

"We've been compromised," Moses said.

Gasps echoed through the room, the nine leaders exchanging glances, no doubt wondering who had blabbed.

"What?" one of the few surviving judges asked. "How?"

"Doesn't matter," Moses said. "We need to evacuate now. Gang bangers are downstairs."

"How did they get past the guards?" the chief asked.

The window imploded, throwing Juli and Moses into the hallway against the tiled wall.

She groaned as she slid to the floor, then coughed out dust. "Moses…"

"Juli!" He tossed aside debris, frantically checked her limbs and palpated her scalp. "Are you hurt? Talk to me!" She grunted.

"Moses," she said, grasping his hand. "I'm ok." She'd be sore tomorrow, but for now adrenaline pumped through her veins, screaming at her to leave.

She groaned as she stood, Moses propelling her up. Her vision swam with black before she realized the conference room where their leaders had been no longer existed, moonlight illuminating the grisly scene.

"Oh no."

The mayor lay in a crumpled heap in the doorway. Juli bent to feel her neck before she noticed the glassy eyed look. "That's it. They're all dead."

Juli straightened, taking in the limbs and other body parts flung against the tile wall she'd hit. How had they survived unscathed?

"…have to go." Moses's words startled Juli.

Gunfire erupted from the northern staircase, and Moses pushed her forward in a headlong sprint back the way they'd come, returning fire down the straight hallway.

They were sitting ducks. And boy, she'd love to know who'd ratted them out. She wasn't a violent person, but if she ever discovered who'd done it, her violence was the least of their worries.

Juli hit the staircase and remembered the night-vision goggles still clutched in her left hand. Exclaiming, she donned them as they vaulted down the stairs, swinging at the landings. Moses darted ahead of her, firing off a round when the first-floor door opened.

They were trapped.

Moses signaled for her to guard the staircase above them as he eased the door open into the hallway, firing blindly. Groans echoed back. The second-floor door crashed open and footsteps thundered down. Juli schooled her pulse and fired at the man whose gaping mouth belied his surprise. Her shots found center mass as another fighter ground to a halt and reversed up the stairs, gunfire pinging off the metal railing.

Moses tugged her into the hallway, vaulting over several bodies as they sprinted around the corner. He lifted a finger to his lips as footsteps echoed after them.

Moses rounded the corner, firing shot after shot until silence reigned. Juli trailed as Moses stripped their weapons, tossing her several handguns including an ancient Colt Python along with extra ammo. She holstered her Beretta, checking the rounds left in the Colt.

"That's it," Moses said, shouldering his backpack. "That's a beauty if I've ever seen one," Moses said, gesturing with his chin to the Colt still in her grip. It reminded her of her father's. "Only good thing to come out of today. Let's try to make it back to the underground tunnels alive."

"Great idea," she said as they exited the courthouse into the pre-dawn light.

Juli pulled her night-vision goggles off, leaving them around her neck. They had no time to spare now that their only remaining leaders were dead. She wondered how they'd unite the militias, when even their city leaders had floundered. What hope did they have of defeating these mega-gangs even if they did unite? And how did these gangs have such immense firepower and bombs?

"Let's use the riverwalk path," Moses said, pulling her southward.

Gunfire echoed through the streets, the sound bouncing off the glass and metal buildings. An explosion rocked the morning, propelling Juli into a headlong sprint. If only they could make it back to their bunker in Over-the-Rhine without getting themselves killed.

Chapter 4: Moses

They'd barely made it back to the underground tunnels in one piece, only to learn that the attack on the federal and city government buildings hadn't been the only fighting that day. Militias around the city reported heavy casualties as drones and gang bangers armed with AR-15s descended on the neighborhood fortifications. Moses had only seen most of the weapons the militias described in Ranger armories or on a *Call of Duty* game. He yearned for an operational helicopter to scout the enemy's position from above, but the enemy owned the skies. How they had working drones — and how they kept them charged — was beyond Moses's know-how.

That fact alone proved there was something much larger at play. The enemy was too coordinated, too well-equipped to not have powerful allies. Moses suspected he'd find national powers behind the mega-gangs, not just the nuclear attacks or the EMP.

"We only have a few more days' clean water supply," Juli said, emerging from the kitchen pantry, her hands on her hips.

"I'll go scavenge the Vine Street Kroger," Moses said at her upraised palm.

"You don't think it'll be ransacked by now? 'Cause I do. We're going to have to figure out how to draw water through the city pipes, Moses. And when are Rev and Matthew returning?" Juli asked. "They've been gone for days now. I miss Angie."

Moses scrubbed a hand down his face. "They're not coming back. Any of them." Weariness filled his soul.

"What?" Juli shouted. "What about all that talk of sticking together and getting the militias to work as one unit?"

"The attacks happened, that's what," Moses said, hunching over in a chair and resting his forehead on his palms. "They lost too many militia fighters. Both of them said they need to train others, consolidate their positions." Moses tilted his head back to examine the ceiling. "They're trying their best, but it won't make a lick of difference. Plus Matthew won't leave Angie."

"How many stayed?"

"Ian left. Donna's still here, as is Isley. But without Ian, Rev and Matthew involved, how can we coordinate movements between the various militias?"

Juli sat across from him, grabbing his hand. They locked gazes.

"Look Moses, I know our friends are busy, but they need help. They're too far apart to collaborate effectively. I have an idea to bring everyone together, but still allow each militia to have their own territory."

Moses shook his head, weariness clouding his thinking. Why couldn't he come up with something? He had the unconventional ops and strategic defense skills, not anyone else in their group. Moses was the only professional soldier in their group. This was his burden to shoulder, not the civilians' burden. Must be the lack of sleep and the weight of grief of realizing he'd never see his Ranger unit again. Hell, he didn't know if they were even alive. He told himself to get it together.

Juli sprinted down the hallway, shouting for the others to meet in the kitchen. She returned with a map of the city and a stack of paper tucked under her arm. Everyone clustered around the table.

"We can do this, Moses," she said as she spread the map on the table. Using a red pen, she marked a two-block radius around the University of Cincinnati. "The dorms can house everyone. Each militia gets one dorm, we defend the perimeter together. Sharpshooters on the rooftops can watch for drones."

Donna pointed to the Tangeman University Center. "The school evacuated, but I bet there's still food for thousands of students stored here and inside the residence hall cafeterias. Plus, maybe we could bring the university power plant back online, if we could only find someone in the city with the skills. This could work."

Others in the group chimed in ideas, from using the large green spaces in the middle of campus to start a vegetable and fruit garden come springtime, to highlighting the world-class workout facility they could use to train new militia fighters.

"But how will we convince the militia to leave their neighborhoods? And how will people survive the summer heat in those dorms?" Moses asked.

"If we survive to the summer, we'll find a way," Juli said, as she drew out a more detailed map of the campus by hand. She'd know, having attended UC for her teaching degree. "Protecting a two-block radius gives us control over another Kroger, the shops along Calhoun, and, if we stretch ourselves, the hospital."

"They hit UC Med," Donna said. "It was on fire the last I saw."

"Crap," Juli said, dropped her pen on the table. "Scratch that. Maybe we can scavenge supplies at the University Student Health Clinic."

"Anyone heard from Rubin across the river?" Moses asked.

"You're not going to like this," Donna said. "Northern Kentucky and Indiana reported the refugees stopped arriving earlier today."

Juli frowned.

"They've surrounded the city," Moses said, his fingers tracing the I-275 circuit around Cincinnati, cutting through Indiana and Kentucky. "It's what I'd do if I could. But how?"

Donna crossed her arms over her chest, biting her lower lip. Moses didn't know her that well, but the large white woman was a force to be reckoned with and their only trained nurse.

"Just tell me."

"According to Jed in Indiana, the mega-gangs have tanks and armored vehicles, Russian Tigrs. Though they don't bear the Russian flag."

"Damn," Moses said, tipping back in his chair. "That explains a whole helluva lot. Russia. China. North Korea. And maybe even Iran. How did we not see this coming? Talk about an intel failure."

The room fell silent. How could their bunch of ragtag fighters defend an entire city against gang bangers backed by the remaining world superpowers and a few rogue states?

"Um, that's not all," Donna said, uncrossing her arms to scratch her ear. "Jed said there's a mass grave in Cleves. Rubin said there's another right by Riverbend Stadium. Moses, they're shooting refugees fleeing south over the bridges. Did you two see anything at the Brent Spence or the Purple People bridge when you were downtown?"

"That was the one remaining escape route since the police controlled downtown and the Guard patrolled the Brent Spence."

"We were running for our lives," Juli said. "There was gunfire everywhere. Echoing off the buildings. I couldn't tell if it was aimed at us or not. And I have to admit I didn't so much as glance at the bridges. Too busy staying alive."

"And once we got to the riverwalk, we were sprinting." Moses closed his eyes and retraced their earlier flight out of downtown. He shook his head. "No. I don't recall fighting on the bridges. If the gangs control those, they either seized them after we escaped or had them under control before we passed."

"Has anyone heard from Alvarez in Price Hill? Did the Mexican militias survive the gang's onslaught?" Juli asked.

Juli's family was from Puerto Rico and Colombia and lived in the county to the north of Cincinnati, but a fellow teacher and other friends lived in the Price Hill community. If Moses let her, she'd probably walk up the hill and check on them. But Moses would never let her endanger herself that way.

Donna frowned. "They never had a radio. And they haven't sent a messenger in days." She wiped her forehead, then brushed her hand on her jeans. "Perhaps we should send someone to check on them?"

He shook his head. "Too dangerous. I'm going on a walkabout. I need to get a lay of the land. Who controls what. If I can get into Price Hill, I'll bring word back." He punched the table. "We should've left while we could. Now we're trapped. Like fish in a barrel."

Moses was also mad at his friends for abandoning efforts to unify the city's militias. It was hard to fault them for wanting to protect their people, but he didn't understand why they refused to combine forces. Alone, they'd be picked off militia by militia. Together, they had a shot at success. Even as well resourced as their enemy was.

Juli gripped his forearm, drawing his eyes to her. "No, we aren't. I'll get on the radio and rally the militia, contact Matthew and Rev and make sure they're alive still. Then talk to Jed and Rubin. Assuming the gangs aren't monitoring those channels, which I don't think we can. We need to come up with a code."

"I'll get on that," Donna said. "I love puzzles. You know we used the Navajo language in World War Two, right? I bet I could write a code using my native Cherokee."

Moses raised his eyebrows. Of course, he'd studied the history of code talkers and code breakers, but never in his life could he imagine he'd need a cipher. And the news that Donna wasn't a hundred percent white Caucasian shouldn't shock him, but it did. As he examined her, he recognized the high cheekbones and broad nose typical of a Cherokee Native.

"Cherokee is perfect if you can teach the other radio operators. They don't have time to learn a new language."

"Oh, I'll do you one better. It won't be actual Cherokee, just a code based on it. And I'll create a cipher we can smuggle to them."

"But that means crossing the river," Juli said. "And if the reports are true, there's no exit from the city."

"You get the militia to come together and leave that to me," Moses said. "There's always a way out for one person."

Juli's answering scowl told him what she thought of that.

And maybe if he could get out of the city, he could convince his bride to escape. They had a child to protect, and he'd do just about anything to make sure they both lived.

Chapter 5: Julianna

Reports of mass graves beyond the 275 boundary horrified Juli, making her hand drift toward her baby bump. At only twelve weeks pregnant, she wasn't really showing yet. At least she could fit into her clothes. None of this changed her protectiveness toward the life within her or her desperation to rid her city of the thugs whose noose slowly tightened around their necks.

Juli marveled as the last of the neighborhood militia, led by Matthew Chen, filtered onto the UC campus under the cover of night. The mega-gangs' attacks and people fleeing for their lives had reduced the city's two-million-plus population to well under ten thousand.

The regular drone attacks on pockets of the remaining population had further weakened militia defenses, and driven many into a suicidal bid for escape. At least those who hadn't already burned to a crisp in the fires that swept across the city as transistors blew after the EMP or who hadn't died in their beds after a home invasion.

And while the National Guard-Cincinnati PD combined forces had prevented the gang's Tigrs from assaulting the large groups heading to the university, gangs had still picked off unit after unit in rapid-fire, coordinated attacks.

She wondered if she'd led the entire city into a trap by gathering everyone here. Had they fallen right into the gangs' strategy?

Juli paced the portico entrance of the College of Law building — which had never been renamed after the law school's move to north campus — nodding at the residents carrying sleeping children and encouraging wounded or older adults dragging tired feet to hurry. The group passed the concrete barrier on Clifton Avenue and followed the leader down shadowed steep steps toward the Asian dorm. Several men eyed her curls and full lips, noting her rifle and holstered Beretta as if calculating if they could take her out before she killed them. She and Moses had assembled a fragile alliance, a powder keg ripe for a spark. The various militias didn't trust one another, having fought against each other almost as hard as they now fought the gangs. But no one could ignore reality any longer.

A Middle Eastern saying came to mind, "The enemy of my enemy is my friend."

What would happen if they couldn't get the university's power plant up and running? If they had to endure the heat of summer or the frigid winter temps in the dorms? Or if they ran out of food?

Thankfully, water wasn't an issue with the Miami Valley aquifer beneath them. National Guard teams had dug wells around campus over the last few days. Their skills amazed Juli. Fighting, digging wells, securing territory, repairing communications. Donna had loved that, having taken over the Guard's secure radio transmission base to coordinate everyone.

A Guard member walked by, the stench of his unwashed body consuming her, reminding her they were still ordinary men and women, despite their skills.

She swallowed the urge to vomit and breathed through her nose, wondering when the scent sensitive stage of pregnancy would end.

At least the man carried an automatic rifle and wore a bulletproof vest as he'd escorted the Vietnamese militia miles through the war zone.

"Moses, where are you?"

He'd left the night before to sneak out of the city and deliver the cipher to Jed and Rubin, assuming the two were still alive. In their last communication, Rubin had reported drone attacks on their positions and that they'd retreated farther away from Cincinnati.

Would Moses find him? Worry for her husband was always at the front of Juli's mind, even in the middle of a gun battle.

"We should plan for a coordinated attack from multiple sides," Rev said as he ascended the law school's steps to join her. He lifted night-vision goggles to his face, scanning the neighborhood in rubble across the street.

"Agreed. Let's assemble the leaders."

"Was that the last of the Asian neighborhoods to evacuate?"

"I think. I hope." Juli ducked into the darker shadows of the columns, shielding her eyes from the waning moon, and scanned the streets.

"Filipinos arrived first." Rev ticked the groups off on his fingers. "Then the remaining Thai community, though too many tried to flee and probably ended up in the mass graves." He scrubbed his face. "Other second-generation Asians who stayed behind and any of the remaining graduate students living in Clifton were already here. Who did we miss?"

He looked exhausted. She felt every bit of that herself.

"You warned the Viet community leader that would happen, but he didn't listen." She tapped her foot and lowered her voice. "Don't beat yourself up about it, *Reverendo*."

Rev turned to face her. "You should be in bed. You know it'll be a few more days before we should send out the search party, right?"

Juli scratched the back of her neck, tucking stray curls away from her face. "I know. It's just that… I don't know. He's skilled and if anyone could get around the roadblocks and checkpoints, it's my Moses. What if they're all dead, though?"

Rev shrugged. "Nothing anyone can do about that. We have to focus on the people we've gathered, those we've been able to save so far. Can't worry about stuff out of our control. Not that we can even control what we're sitting on top of."

He slung an arm around her shoulders and squeezed, turning her back toward the center of campus. "Go get some sleep. We'll gather the leaders in the morning and set a plan. I don't think they'll attack tonight."

"Matthew's IEDs will keep them busy."

Rev harrumphed. "I hope we hear the explosions. It'll be music to my ears."

As Rev had escorted the last of the Asian ethnic militias and their families to the university, Matthew's team had planted small improvised explosive devices in a defensive ring. Before Moses had left, he'd taught Matthew and a group of engineers how to assemble the IEDs. Though similar bombs had wreaked havoc in Iraq and Afghanistan, they could be what kept the gangs at bay in Cincinnati for now. Hopefully long enough to figure out a solid defense plan or how to move thousands out of the city without everyone ending up dead or captive.

The engineers had worked around the clock in the College of Engineering maker space, having found a working generator. They'd had too much fun building the bombs. Why such talented men and women had stayed behind when the power went out mystified her. Then again, she and Moses were still here.

With Matthew and Angie with them again, Juli had a friend to lean on. She'd spent hours with Angie, the two talking about baby things and searching the university library for books on pregnancy, childbirth and child-rearing. Juli had no clue what to expect, and neither did Angie, who was already four months pregnant. They both were doing this without their families around, which saddened Juli.

A shout echoed up from the magnet tech high school across the street. Juli clutched her rifle to her chest and peered into the darkness.

Rev backed into deeper shadows as they monitored the garage attached to the high school.

Gunfire filled the air.

"Don't move," he said from behind another pillar. "Disperse the mist from your breath. Someone's posted over there, right?"

"Affirmative." Juli tucked her chin into her jacket collar, breathing in and out through her nose as she waited for the attack to penetrate past their perimeter guard.

Screams of pain followed more gunfire.

"Damn. Do you think they got our sentry?"

"I hope not."

A group of smaller figures sprinted away from the garage's lower level and onto Clifton Avenue.

Rev emerged into the moonlight, waving for them to come toward him.

"Hurry!" a woman cried out as they ran.

Another round of gunfire echoed out of the garage, and the woman catapulted forward onto the road.

"Mom!" a tall, gangly boy yelled. His bright blond hair was like a lamp reflecting the moonlight.

Juli dashed from behind the pillar, her rifle trained on the darkened parking garage. She fired at a darker shadow, a grunt her only reward for successfully reaching the screaming child. Rev gathered the six other children, leading them toward the law school portico and safety.

She wrapped her free hand around the teen's shoulders, turning him away from the pool of blood spreading beneath his mother. "Come on, *hijo*. We have to leave or the bad men will kill us."

"But my mom…" he sputtered, looking back as she tugged him toward the university and the rest of his family.

"Take them inside," Rev said when Juli joined him behind the pillar. "I'm going to investigate."

"No, wait for me. Don't go alone. That's insane."

"That was my man in there. I have to see…"

She gripped his bicep and gestured to the kids. "No, Rev. Help me get them to safety, then I'll go with you. They aren't attacking now. He must've dealt with them and is behind his barricade again."

Rev's full beard twitched, and Juli held her breath. She didn't want to lose another leader. "Alright."

Juli's shoulders relaxed. They herded the children toward the steps to Backstage Alley, wondering how they'd missed a white family with all these kids in their neighborhood canvasses. She also wondered who would care for seven orphaned kids.

Chapter 6: Moses

Moses employed all his Ranger talents to slip away from Cincinnati, and finally, he found an opening when a sentry dozed off. A sleeping sentry. Otherwise, their defenses were tight.

He'd checked roads crossing over or under the 275 ring from Montgomery to Colerain. Every one of them had a blockade with a group of heavily armed gang bangers and those Russian Tigrs. If he previously doubted that powerful nations were behind their nation's demise before, he no longer did.

Add to that the shoulder-mounted RPGs that looked suspiciously similar to the People's Army of China's and the black uniforms with heavy combat boots. The mega-gangs had morphed into an army.

He shook his head. He couldn't do a damn thing about that. Command was in disarray, maybe even dead. They hadn't heard from their contacts in the Cincinnati National Guard in days. Forget Metro PD. He'd had to circle extra-wide to avoid the mega-gangs surrounding the PD's last operational command facility in Norwood.

PD put up a hearty defense, but wouldn't last long against the gangs' overwhelming firepower.

Moses stopped along the tree-lined creekside to gain his bearings. He pulled out the worn map, tracing his route ahead by the wan moonlight. He'd see better with the rising sun, but lose the cover of darkness.

Jed and his people had holed up in a retreat center deep in the woods outside Brookville, Indiana. Far off the main roadways, they'd gathered hundreds, if not thousands, of locals to shelter at the sprawling property.

The outcome of this fight seemed inevitable. Moses needed to preserve as many lives as possible, convincing people to flee to refuge in Canada or south across the Mexican border. Moses hated that their only hope was leaving homes and nation behind.

An hour later, Moses whistled the "safe" signal to the sentry posted in the thick scrub off the dirt road of Jed's property. The woman stepped out of the undergrowth after whistling her reply, waving him in with her rifle. He nodded as he passed, pleased she had green and brown camouflage clothing, perfect for their midwestern woods, and black paint obscured her features. Her crisp salute startled him.

"Where did you serve?" he asked.

"Navy, sir," she replied.

"Thank you for your service and I'm glad you escaped the onslaught our naval forces suffered."

"I've been out four years, sir."

Moses nodded and, at her direction, walked down the dirt road toward the massive red wood barn, passing more guards along the way. Jed's setup impressed Moses.

"Moses Reynolds," he said, extending a hand to the guard at the barn door.

The man shook his hand and gestured for Moses to enter.

"Moses!" Jed's booming bass thundered in the cavernous space.

A bear-sized man wrapped him in a hug. Moses wasn't small at six foot three inches and two hundred eighty pounds of muscle, but the former pro linebacker dwarfed him. Immediately after the first nuclear attacks, local leaders in Indiana had pulled Jed into their defense planning. Moses had met Jed, and the former Army captain and National Guardsman Rubin, in his work training police departments and assisting townships with civil defense measures. Little had they known that within weeks, their friendship would become mission-critical.

"Excellent setup here," Moses said.

"Did they follow protocol? I've got a few army types who set up everything." Jed ran a hand over his thick beard, stroking its long ends. "Figured you'd tell me how competent they are."

"They've done good."

Jed gestured for Moses to sit in one of the chairs strewn haphazardly around what must've been the farm office space. The barn smelled of hay and horse manure, reflecting the beasts' occupancy over the years, though they weren't there now. For all Moses knew, they were in a pasture somewhere. A dog growing up was the extent of Moses's animal knowledge.

"How was your journey?" Jed asked.

Moses shook his head. "This is much bigger than we thought." Moses rested his forehead against his palms. "They've got Russian, Chinese and North Korean armaments, equipment, vehicles, and who knows what else. I hardly escaped the city, except for a slumbering guard. I don't see how we're getting out of this. We're trapped."

Jed shot to his feet. "Can't we get help? Join forces for a coordinated attack to bust y'all out?"

"And go where?" Moses shouted, clenching his hands into tight fists. "We'd be dead in minutes. They have helicopters, Tigrs and who knows what else. We're easy pickings."

Jed planted his fists onto his hips and stared out of the dusty office window. Accumulated dirt lined his face, accentuating the man's obvious lack of sleep and a shower over the past few days. Moses wondered how these people fed themselves. He hadn't seen the mega-gang patrols in nearly fifty miles, but they'd come, eventually. Once they had the city secured.

Moses joined Jed, crossing his arms over his chest. "You should take your people and run to Canada, Jed."

Jed whipped a sharp gaze toward Moses.

"And abandon you here?" Jed shook his head and looked away again, focusing on the wall opposite the office.

Moses faced Jed and gripped his friend's shoulder. "We have no chance. They'll smoke us out, take us prisoner, I don't know. I hope we survive. But you? They aren't paying attention to the countryside yet. Yet." His lifted hand silenced Jed's protest. "Listen. This is classic. They'll secure the city. Then, one by one, clear the towns and rural areas. Don't think they'll leave you alone out here. They'll come and by then, what resources will you still have? How will you flee with an army chasing you? Leave now. While you can."

Jed lifted his face toward the ceiling and growled. "Damn them."

"I know. I feel those same things. But my feelings don't change reality. I can hate this all I want, but I still need to do what's best for my people."

"What will you do?"

"Convince you and Rubin to take your people elsewhere. Hell, I don't care where. Canada or Mexico. A hole in the ground. Anywhere but around these big cities. I'd like to think someone somewhere in the continental US is winning the fight, but after they decimated our PD and Guard, I doubt it."

"No, Moses," Jed said, a finger pointing into his chest. "What are *you* going to do? You've got a baby on the way. Join us. Sneak Juli out. Come with us. Help us get to Canada without dying."

Moses paced the small office, the offer more tempting than he'd admit. Then, he remembered the stream of families, men and women who'd waited too long to flee or who didn't have the resources to try. The children playing soccer on the wide grass field at the university, delighted to be out in the sunshine.

He stopped in front of Jed. "No can do. I'll figure out a way to keep them alive. Somehow."

Jed sighed. "At least stay the day before heading to Rubin. He's moved again."

"That reminds me. Donna will kill me if I forget to give you this." Moses dug the cipher out of his backpack, handing it to Jed.

His friend examined it and boomed out a laugh. "Brilliant! What language is this?"

"Donna speaks fluent Cherokee, so she based the cipher on that," he said, wiping the sweat from his brow onto his dusty pants leg. "Smarter than me, that's for sure."

Jed carefully folded the paper. "Let's find you a bed and some chow. We're preserving the lake as our water source and haven't worked out how to empty the septic tank yet, so no showers. Sorry."

Moses shrugged. "I stink, but it can't be as bad as Iraq."

"Or two-a-days. I get it." Jed wrapped an arm around Moses' shoulders and guided him into the barn loft.

"I'll send someone up with breakfast, but grab some shut-eye while I take this to our communications team."

"Thank you, Jed," Moses said, pausing with one foot on the ladder. "I'm sorry it's come to this."

"Not your fault," Jed said. "In fact, I doubt we would've lasted as long as we did without your foresight and training."

"Doesn't change the thousands in mass graves outside the 275 corridor."

Jed blinked several times, his jaw clenching. "Thousands? I hadn't heard there were that many. All those people."

"At every major intersection. Those people were sitting ducks against the mega-gang's firepower."

"Damn. That could be us." Jed took a deep breath, his gaze turned toward the bright light outside. "Get some rest, my friend. I'll gather our leaders. Make a plan to hightail it out of here."

Jed strode out of the barn. Moses watched him go, knowing how he felt. Every one of those lives hung on Moses's conscience. They should've seen this coming. "They" meaning the intelligence community, the military command, someone. He climbed the ladder and collapsed onto the hay.

Several hours later, Moses bolted upright at a hand on his shoulder, nearly knocking his head into Jed's.

"Whoa there," Jed said, scooting backward. "Remind me to shout first. That's what I get for trying to be nice."

"Sorry, chock that up to the military. What's up?"

"Rubin's moved yet again," he said, handing Moses an index card with an address and directions printed in a careful hand. "Radioed just now. But Moses, they're monitoring our channels. Have to be. Rubin said he'd just gotten settled in a new warehouse when sentries spotted gang patrols blocks away. They need that cipher. I hate to ask this, but…"

"I'll sleep later," Moses said as he rose to his feet, crouching when his head grazed the barn's ceiling joists. He noticed the tray containing thick oatmeal and slices of bacon. "Whoever delivered that needs to be on sentry or scout duty. Dang, I didn't even hear them."

Jed smiled. "That would be my wife, and no way I'm putting her on either. That's what years of tiptoeing around sleeping children will do for stealth training."

Moses inhaled the meal, not caring in the slightest about the quality or temperature. Bacon tasted just as great cold as hot in his humble opinion. Calories were calories. And he needed plenty for his journey.

"Any wisdom on crossing the Ohio?" Moses asked as he joined Jed at the bottom of the ladder.

"Follow those directions. There's this place on the river, a few miles downstream from the 275 bridge in Aurora. Lots of people had boats docked there. You should be able to find a way across that's not electric-powered. Do you sail?"

Moses snorted out a laugh. "You gotta be kidding me. Who do I look like? Some New England Kennedy wanna be? Remember, I was Army? And for a good reason. Water is meant for drinking and bathing and nothing else."

Jed grinned. "Maybe you'll be lucky and something at that dock still runs."

"God, I hope so, too. Swimming isn't a viable option. Though, don't get me wrong, I can swim."

Jed walked out of the barn, Moses trailing him. A petite Filipina woman joined them, Jed planting a gentle kiss on the woman's cheek.

"This is my wife, Selene. Baby, this is Moses."

She dipped her head and gave him a sandwich wrapped in a thin towel. "That should help you get to the river without your stomach eating through your spine, Moses."

"How do you know me so well and we've only just met?" Moses asked, winking at Jed.

Selene patted her husband's chest with a grin. "You're cut from the same cloth, the two of you. Godspeed Moses."

Jed wrapped an arm around Selene, pulling her into his side as Moses thanked them both.

"Be careful, Moses," Jed said.

"You, too, my friend. And stay in touch. We'll need to know how to send people to you if we can get them out."

"You bet." Jed watched Moses walk away, hand held up in a wave, which Moses returned. It would probably be their last time seeing one another, which saddened him.

That evening a few miles downstream from Aurora and as the setting sun blinded him, Moses stared at a dilapidated rowboat. He gritted his teeth at the task ahead of him and pushed away from the dock. The only bright spot was that it hadn't rained in days. Perhaps the Ohio wouldn't be a cruel master tonight.

Chapter 7: Julianna

Juli paced the candlelit communications hub behind Donna. Her colleague had headphones on and frantically transcribed a message using their new cipher. Beside her, Ian chewed his thumbnail and peered over Donna's shoulder, watching her work.

"How are they doing this?" he mumbled.

Juli shrugged. Earlier that day, Donna had told her Moses had arrived safely at Jed's farm and was resting comfortably before the next leg of his journey. Donna had chuckled, sharing how the radio operator in Indiana had sent random messages to practice their new cipher. When Juli learned Jed and his team were heading for Canada, she'd felt the loss down to her toes, despite never having met the man face-to-face. She was certain Rubin and his people would make the same decision after having to move yet again.

She'd never felt so alone in her life. Juli wondered where her parents and siblings were. Her ex-military father would surely have taken the family to a safer place if he could convince her headstrong brother to leave his newly bought home. That is, if they'd survived the post-EMP mega-gang attacks all the way up in Fairfield Township. Maybe their area had been unaffected. Juli cringed at her wishful thinking. Of course, the gangs had probably left no suburb untouched.

She doubted she'd ever see her family again on this side of heaven. She felt her mood spiral downward at the familiar thought that her parents would never meet their grandchild.

Ian's groan, followed by a fist slamming into the table, jostling the candles and Donna's water cup, snapped Juli back to reality.

"They're surrounded and out of ammo," Donna said.

"Who?" Juli asked. "Who's surrounded?" She prayed it wasn't Rubin, though she didn't see how they'd have the cipher this soon. Maybe Moses had traveled far faster than expected.

"The Norwood PD station," Donna said, handing her the message.

Ammo gone. Tigrs blocking all routes out. Hostiles entering building. Last transmission. Keep fighting. Remember us.

Juli collapsed, almost missing the rolling chair.

"We're alone. That's it," she whispered.

"Damn it. Raise Matthew and Rev," Ian ordered, jostling Juli out of her despair. "They'll be coming here next."

Donna relayed the brief message on their open channel, using their new cipher. Matthew's voice rang out.

"Backup needed at Corry gate!" he shouted.

The blood drained from her face as she heard the tell-tale rat-a-tat-tat echoing through the room.

Ian grabbed the microphone from Donna, shouting orders to move residents into one building at the center of campus.

Juli gripped Ian's arm. "Stop. We need to evacuate whoever can make the overland trek and river crossing. Go join Rubin or find a cave in the Appalachians to hole up in. They're going to kill us all. Or worse. Make us prisoners."

"But we can defend a smaller area," Ian said.

"What will we do when they send the drones again?" Donna asked. "Juli's right. We need to evacuate as many as we can. And Ian, if Moses isn't back in time, you'll have to lead them. You're the next best survivalist here. Let's give people a fighting chance."

Ian shook his head and crossed his arms over his chest. "I'm not done, though."

"Donna's right," Juli said. "You're the only one who could get a group safely across the river and into hiding someplace. Take a radio. Stay in touch."

Ian exhaled loudly and looked up at the ceiling, his eyes closed. Juli didn't dare breathe in that moment, silently urging him to agree. It was the only way.

"Ok. I'll do it."

She grabbed Ian into a fierce hug, Donna joining on his other side.

"Alright, alright," Ian said. "Stop smothering me. I get it. You're happy."

"Thank you, Ian," Donna said, shifting her gaze to Juli. "Now, what next?"

"Who else knows the cipher, Donna?" Juli asked.

"Ariana and Toby," Donna said, pointing to two teenagers hiding in the shadows that Juli had hardly noted. "Take over for me. I need to help organize an evacuation. Do either of you want to go?"

Juli looked up at the young light-skinned Black teen, noting how he'd probably eclipse her Moses in height and weight once full-grown. She missed watching kids go through the awkward lanky stage, growing like beans overnight. She wondered if she'd ever teach high school again.

Toby shook his head. "My mom can't leave with her broken leg. So I won't, either."

Juli blinked at the idea of a middle-aged woman on crutches in this mess. She thought she had it rough being pregnant. That was an impossible situation. Juli admired Toby for sticking with his mother when she couldn't flee to safety.

"I'll go, for sure," Ari said. "I have nothing and no one keeping me here."

"Ok, then. Ari, you're with Juli and me. Let's sort out who can make a break for it and who will stay."

Ari followed Donna and Juli out of the room, Ian dictating messages for Toby to send.

"We should split up. Cover more ground that way," Juli said as they exited the communications room in the bowels of Tangeman University Center, otherwise known as TUC by students.

"Agreed," Donna said. "Ari, you go with Juli to Calhoun. I'll head to Daniels and Dabney."

Juli waved goodbye, tugging Ari toward one of the larger dormitories on campus and the site of their commissary. For days, teams had gone back and forth to the restaurants and stores along Calhoun and McMillan Streets and cleared out the empty dorms, scavenging anything worth saving. They had a decent stockpile of clothing, non-perishable foods, household items like sheets and towels, and candy to keep the kids in line. Most people arrived at the university with nothing but the clothes on their backs. The Daniels commissary was their first stop before the room assignment coordinator.

"Mrs. Reynolds, are we going to survive?" Ari asked, her footsteps light beside Juli as they walked toward Daniels.

Juli halted on the concrete Veterans Bridge into the music school and faced Ari, gripping the teen's arms. She shoved her own loss and isolation deep down in her soul and dredged up the little spark of hope still left in her heart. Juli had to be strong for Ari and everyone else. This wasn't the time to shrink into a ball of tears in a corner.

"I don't know. But we have to try. Especially you. If anyone can make it, it'll be you young people. You're in great shape, can walk or run for miles. You're smart. We just have to figure out how to get you across that river."

"I'm scared of it," Ari said. "I can swim, but only in a pool. Will we have to swim?"

"Dear Lord, I hope not," Juli whispered. She let her arms fall away.

But the girl was alone now, her parents killed trying to reach the university from nearby Price Hill. What was left of Cincinnati's Mexican population lived in Dabney Hall at the university. So much loss. Too much.

She wrapped an arm loosely around Ari's shoulders, drawing her toward the concrete staircase down into CCM Circle. This part of campus used to be filled with students, music echoing around the space as students practiced instruments in rooms overhead. At the first sign of mass rioting, the university had evacuated students, moving classes online. And good thing, since students had been home when the EMP hit. A college education was now a thing of the past.

They crossed the circle, their footsteps the only sound. Sentries outside Siddall Hall nodded to Juli as they passed, the darkness of deep nighttime shadows surrounding them as they made the last turn into Calhoun Hall. Juli ran a hand along the brick wall. The other gripped Ari's wrist.

She whistled the "safe" code and waited for the sentry's return whistle. When it came, Juli stepped into the moonlight.

"Gather every ethnic group's leaders," she commanded. "We meet in the market in ten minutes."

The taller sentry snapped an "Ok" at her before sprinting into the building, switching on his flashlight.

They were conserving batteries for emergencies, but this qualified.

"Let's head inside and light candles, if they aren't already lit," Juli said.

"Why would they be lit?"

Juli checked her watch. "It's nearly dawn. Today's breakfast crew will be hard at work."

The survivors had worked out a rotation for every duty on the campus, including meals. She hated that they'd only just gotten things settled into a routine here. Evacuating residents would upend routines and any idea of a return to normalcy. But the alternative — dying — was unacceptable.

Juli entered the market's kitchen, smiling at the Hispanic woman kneading dough on a large metal surface.

Juli introduced herself to the woman, settling in to watch her shape the dough into little horns, or *cuernitos*, a traditional Mexican pastry topped with cinnamon and sugar. "Where did you find lard?" Juli asked.

The woman laughed. "Oh, I didn't. Using butter instead is okay. Not great, but it's wartime." She wiped her forehead with her sleeve and gestured over her shoulder. "I'm Maria, by the way. Go get one before the kids eat them all."

Juli groaned at the thought of the light croissant-shaped Mexican pastry, but knew if she put it into her mouth, she'd vomit. Early pregnancy had been easy so far, except for the morning sickness. Which was especially problematic after staying up all night.

Her stomach heaved then growled, making Ari giggle next to her.

"You go ahead," Juli said. "The baby doesn't like food before noon."

Maria wiped her hands on her apron and wrapped several steaming *cuernitos* into a paper towel and handed it to Ari. "Make sure she eats this later since *el bebito* won't let her now. And take a few for yourself."

"*Gracias,*" Juli said with a smile. "For doing this, for being here, for serving us." She looked away as tears filled her eyes.

Maria grabbed Juli into a tight hug, the woman's head pressed into Juli's chest. Juli caved inward to shelter her sensitive bosom and to lower herself to the woman's height. Juli was tall for a Hispanic woman, though Moses dwarfed her.

"Leaders will meet in the cafeteria shortly," Juli said.

"Then we'll bring out a spread when the bacon is ready."

"Did someone say 'bacon'?" Matthew's baritone voice boomed through the kitchen.

"Yes," Maria said as she intercepted him, her body blocking the massive ovens and her fists thrust onto her hips. "It's not ready yet."

Matthew backed away with hands raised. "Sorry! I heard 'bacon' and everything else faded away."

"Good to see you're in one piece, *amigo*," Juli said, following Matthew out of the kitchen.

"It was so amazing. They were attacking our position, one of those Tigrs approaching down MLK when they hit an IED. Kaboom! Decimated the Tigr, and the tide of the battle turned. We chased them up Vine for a block before I pulled everyone back. Ian told me to get my butt here, so I obeyed." He chuckled and wiped dusty hands onto even dustier pants.

"Glad you're still with us," Juli said. "That was a close one. Is the team replacing the IED?"

"Of course," Matthew said, claiming a table at the far end of the cafeteria. "What's this all about?"

Juli eyed Ari, who nodded and went to greet the other leaders.

"That bad, huh?"

Juli took a deep breath and wished she didn't have to tell him they were on their own.

Chapter 8: Moses

Moses jogged along a darkening McMillan Street, turning north as he neared the university. His bones ached, and he longed for his bed, exhaustion saturating every fiber of his being.

He'd found Rubin just as his group was leaving their last known location, patrols from the mega-gangs blocks away. They were heading into the mountains of southeastern Kentucky. Rubin knew of an old cave system used for bluegrass music broadcasts and had decided the deep-cut valleys were more defensible than anything they'd find in the northern Kentucky suburbs. Moses had given Rubin the cipher, encouraging him to keep in touch, stopping himself from counting the few heads that streamed past him into the daylight.

He prayed they would survive. Or that some would. Loss had become inevitable in their world. Moses forced away thoughts of his thug little brother, Corey, his only remaining family. Maybe he'd died in the fighting. He couldn't change Corey's choices now. He'd made his bed years ago, despite Moses's entreaties to join the military.

Twilight had descended on Cincinnati, softening the signs of battle into a haze of blurred edges that became shadows. He wondered who would scrub the city clean of the stains of war and how long it would take them to do it.

He sounded the nightingale call and waited for the echoing whistle. He emerged into the wan moonlight and navigated the elaborate roadblock his team had designed for each of the entry points onto the university. Useless cars, appliances and fencing formed an intricate gate, exposing anyone who approached to concealed snipers in roosts high above and armed sentries at the street level.

"Welcome back, my friend," Rev said, wrapping Moses in a tight hug and slapping his back hard. "Your wife missed you." Moses had missed his friend, too. Reverend Thompson, who used to be a well-known pastor in the city and whom he'd nicknamed "Rev," had become far more than a collaborator in the last few weeks. Rev was family.

An Asian sentry posted up behind a dysfunctional refrigerator huffed out a laugh and rolled her eyes. "She drove us all nuts, in the best way, asking if you'd shown up yet."

His Juli was often a little too free with her emotions. Moses chuckled at the image.

"I missed her too," Moses said. "But she didn't need to worry. Slipping in and out of the city wasn't easy, but it was possible. Where is she?"

"Oh-ho, you'll have to hold your horses on that," Rev said with a sly twist of his mouth. "As soon as you set foot on this campus, the leaders want to meet. There've been developments."

"Alright," Moses said, following Rev away from the Calhoun gate and into the massive dormitory lobby. "Let's get this over with."

"The others may regret their haste after they smell you."

Moses scrubbed a hand down his face. He stunk like the Ohio River. Apt because he'd fallen in not once, but twice. He swore the sewage treatment plants upstream had released everything straight into the river. He was no biologist but figured the river biome wouldn't recover for years, assuming something worse didn't happen.

Rev directed him into the market under Calhoun Hall. As he entered, Juli drew his eyes like a moth to the flame. Because that's what she was — his flame.

Her smile lit a fire inside him. Dang, he'd sorely missed her. She threw herself out of the chair and into his arms.

"Ew!" she yelled into his chest, his river scent erupting like a cloud. She fled the room, hands cupped over her mouth until she reached the trash can in the hallway.

He trailed her by a few feet, not wanting to upset her stomach again. "Sorry. The river's polluted, obviously."

"It's ok," she replied in a nasal voice in between dry heaves.

A few minutes later, she stood, bracing herself on the sides of the trash can. "Ok. I'm ok now. Wow, you stink." She faced him. "I can still smell you from over here," she said as she covered her mouth and nose with her sweatshirt. "I will never forget it as long as I live."

Moses thought he heard her say "*muerta*" under her breath in Spanish and couldn't agree more. His smell could kill someone, for sure.

"Maybe I should shower?" Moses asked the room.

Matthew and Ian both shrugged, while Angie, Donna and Juli all nodded, Angie's eyes so wide it made him laugh.

"I'll go up to the second floor if someone can grab my clothes," Moses said.

Donna shot to her feet. "Let me warn the residents."

They'd divided up the population into floors by ethnicity, but honestly Moses had forgotten who was where.

"I'll get a change of clothes," Juli said, heading toward the stairs.

So they were staying in this building. Made sense. Juli would know he'd want to be nearby the front lines and the communications hub. He'd bet they were on one of the lower floors, too, since Juli despised stair workouts.

A quick ten minutes later, Moses was freshly show-ered, his river-and-sewage-soaked clothing having met its fiery end. He joined Juli as she leaned in to give him a deep sniff.

"Ah, much better."

Juli snuggled into his side. He couldn't agree more.

"How are Rubin and Jed and their people?" Matthew asked, leaning his elbows onto the table.

Moses frowned. "You haven't heard? I thought for sure you'd know more than me."

Matthew lifted a shoulder and gestured with his palms up for Moses to continue.

"Jed and his folks were leaving the day after me for Canada. Or as far as they could make it." Moses shifted closer to his Velcroed-to-his-side wife. "And Rubin barely made it out of their latest digs alive. They were literally heading for the hills."

Moses didn't go into detail. He was beginning to suspect that the walls here had ears. Like how the gangs had found out Rubin's location so fast.

"How did you get in and out? How are their defenses structured?" Ian asked.

Moses grabbed a piece of paper from a stack in the center and drew the barricades at every major road crossing the 275 corridor.

"Here," Moses said gesturing to the riot fencing. "These are mobile. The concrete barriers less mobile, but my guess is they have the equipment to pull it off. They can just work these barriers inward, tightening the noose around the city. It'll take them a week, maybe ten days, far as I can tell."

"We're doomed," Donna said, dropping her head into her hands.

"Maybe not," Ian said, coming around the table to stand beside Moses. He grabbed the folded Cincinnati map out of the center of the table and opened it. "See here. When they start moving the barricades, it'll create a window of opportunity on side streets like these. Assuming they don't have those under patrol, which they'd be nuts not to, you could still work your way around the barricades. Then, wait for patrols to pass on 275 and up and over you go. It'll take patience and absolute quiet, but we could get small groups out."

Ian stood to his full height and flipped his ball cap backward. "I'm willing to try. We have to. All these people." He heaved out a breath and eyed the group gathered.

Approaching footsteps sent Moses shooting to his feet.

"Who is interrupting this meeting?" Matthew asked, a scowl on his face as he eyed the teenager.

"What's up, Toby?" Ian asked, rising to his feet.

"That's the new radio operator," Juli said, tipping her head toward the young man.

Toby and Ian exchanged a whispered conversation, Ian's pale face losing its color as everyone strained to catch Toby's whispers.

Ian stared at the retreating Toby, Ian's hand braced against a nearby pillar.

"Evidently, we received a message from a man calling himself 'El Paco.'"

"The Cop? What in the world?" Juli muttered.

Ian collapsed into the chair, unaware he'd almost ended up on the floor.

"They have one of our men," Ian began. "They must've tortured him, because this Paco guy is demanding to speak with you, Moses." Ian's gaze lifted and connected with Moses's.

And for the first time in his life, even counting his tours as an Army Ranger, Moses felt the grip of fear on his soul. Fear not for himself, but for Juli and their child. If this *mafioso* knew Moses led the group, then surely he knew about Juli, as well. His face heated and a cool hand covered his clenched fists.

"It doesn't mean anything," Juli said, patting his fist. "So he knows your name. He doesn't know who you are. We need you to help our people flee. He may never get to you, Moses. You could be three states away by the time they penetrate our defenses."

Moses shook his head, clarity cutting through the fog of reality. He would escort as many people as possible out of the city. But ultimately there were other things more valuable than his safety.

Chapter 9: Julianna

Juli wrapped a thin blanket around her shoulders and gazed out at the starlit pre-dawn sky. Her husband was back, but she sensed a new restlessness in him. An impatience she didn't understand. He'd collapsed and slept like the dead. She supposed he'd barely stopped in the week he'd been gone. She hadn't slept much either, worry sending her pacing and planning. Pacing and planning, like some never-ending hamster wheel.

Warm hands gripped her shoulders and pulled her against a hard chest. She relaxed into Moses's strength. How could she ever go on without him? And if he kept taking risks like crossing the Ohio River alone, Juli feared she'd lose him for good.

Tears pricked her eyes, and she blinked rapidly to stop them from falling. She had to be strong for him this time. If he saw her crying, he'd come unglued.

"I don't like it," she said.

"I think you've expressed that, but it's the only way. We can't let this Paco guy get everyone. We have to save as many as we can."

"I know. I don't want to leave without you." She spun to rest her cheek against his chest, allowing him to cradle her head in his enormous hands. "What if we're separated? How will Ian connect with Rubin without the radio? We should take one."

"I think we have a mole."

Juli drew back with a gasp, cold air filling the space between them and chilling her to the core. "Wha — ?"

"The gangs caught up to Rubin too fast every time he moved. Which is why he went radio silent and will continue until we ferret out who the mole is. Which means they probably know the new cipher."

Juli palmed her forehead. How could they survive this? Their enemy was too well equipped, too well armed, and too sneaky. How had they infiltrated their leadership ranks? Few people knew the cipher existed. Who could the mole be?

"If we have a mole, then we have an even bigger problem, Moses." Juli stepped away, folding her arms over her chest and hugging the blanket tighter around her. "Think about it."

"Oh, I have."

"Three operators know the cipher here, plus Jed's and Rubin's operators." Juli ticked off the fingers on one hand to reach five. "Then you have our leadership team. Ian, Matthew, Angie, Rev, Donna, you, and me. That's it. I can't imagine anyone on Rubin's team being the mole, since that would endanger their life. And you met Jed's. Which leaves someone here."

"I don't think it's Rubin's or Jed's operators. Each time Rubin's group had to move, it was within an hour of them transmitting their new position to us. After that happening twice, they experimented and didn't tell us until the next day. And that's when the gangs arrived. But they told Jed before leaving. That eliminates Jed's and Rubin's operators. Narrows our pool. Two operators here and our leaders."

"I trust Rev with my life and Donna worked hard on that cipher. Ian is leading teams. It couldn't be him, right?"

Moses shrugged. "It's not Angie. She never leaves the university and doesn't have access to the communications hub. It's as likely to be Matthew or one of the radio guys here. How well do you know those kids?"

"Hardly at all. One's a teenager, barely old enough to shave, whose mother has a broken leg. That's Toby, the young man who delivered the message from El Paco demanding your surrender. The other is a young woman named Ari. She lost her entire family in the attacks on Price Hill, but was a senior at Walnut before everything. Bright girl."

She leaned against the cool window glass, wracking her brain. Why hadn't they seen this coming? The gangs had captured and tortured a man, but he didn't know the cipher. They'd limited that to a handful of people, for just this reason. This was a puzzle for later, when she was well rested.

"I want to go with you," Juli said.

"I don't think —"

"Wait and listen before reacting. I can't imagine my life without you. I don't want to bring up our child alone. How could I? Moses, I can't." The tears she'd held at bay now streamed down her face. "What do you want me to do, go to the mountains and raise our son or daughter on my own if they capture or kill you? I don't know I'd survive getting out of the city, forget making it to the mountains on foot! I'd rather face whatever comes together."

Moses turned away from her. "We decided this. All of us. You're staying here to get everyone organized. Ian and I will lead the groups and you'll go with his last group. It's for the best."

He grabbed her into a hug. "Please, don't fight this. If they capture you and I'm alive, I don't know what I'd do. This way, we aren't together, so maybe they won't know who you are if they capture you." He stepped back, gripping her upper arms and bending to look her in the eyes. "You worry about me, but do you actually think I'm strong enough to bear it if they captured you? Do you want to know what I think will happen in our nation?"

Juli blinked at him, stunned into silence.

"I think this El Paco guy, or whoever he works for, will set up his own government. The way our enemies outfitted him, they have a plan for the USA, and it's not us descending into chaos or killing everyone. I think they want to preserve a base population for their own reasons. Maybe they'll make us slaves. Or maybe, just maybe, they'll set up villages or towns, and life will go on. Children will be born and grow up. Families will celebrate birthdays again. Food will be produced and sold. We'll trade with our new allies, who used to be our enemies. And then, maybe, just maybe, you or I will find an opportunity to overthrow them and get our country back."

Juli breathed deeply.

"And, as long as I can figure out how to survive El Paco's vendetta, I'll be there with you every step of the way. Whether we're in the mountains or in a city, we're going to raise our child together. You'll be an outstanding mother, and I intend to see it firsthand."

Juli dove into Moses's arms, burying her face in his muscular chest. She loved his optimistic view of their future. Maybe it was this sense of impending doom that prevented Juli from getting too excited about Moses's grand plans. For now, her plan was to survive today.

Chapter 10: Moses

Moses held out a hand for the group behind him to stop. So far tonight, Moses had guided four other groups to safety beyond the tightening noose of Martin's forces. Barricades moved, distracting the gang bangers, and they'd walked out without incident. This was his last group. His most important group. The one Juli had joined. Because he couldn't deny her when she'd begged him.

But his success streak was ending, as hostiles took up positions both at the next intersection and behind them. The others halted at his signal, sinking into the deep shadows cast from the apartment buildings on either side of this narrow alleyway.

They were trapped. Surrounded.

Had the gangs known of their escape the entire time, waiting for an opportunity to capture Moses? But how had they tracked them? The teens and adults with him had remained utterly silent, except for a rare scuff of a shoe or whisper of clothing. Certainly nothing loud enough to even hear half a block away.

"Freeze!" a male voice boomed out of an old-style megaphone.

Rustling to his rear alerted him to his wife's approach.

"I said freeze!" the man yelled, anger seeping into his tone.

Moses tucked Juli behind him.

"What are you doing? Stay back with the others. I'll handle this. They obviously have night-vision goggles."

"I need you. We have to escape."

"We are looking for Moses. A former military officer. Surrender him and everyone else will live."

Juli's hand tightened on his bicep and he wrapped an arm around her to tuck her tightly to him, still shielding her with his body. His heart broke with what he'd have to do in the next few minutes, but Moses saw no other option.

"No way. Don't surrender!" Juli's whisper-shout gripped his soul.

Moses heard several of the young girls in their group crying softly. Ari's gentle voice joined them. He had to keep them safe. They were his to protect.

He turned and pushed Juli away into Ari's waiting arms. The teenager had refused to leave Juli's side. Ari nodded at him as she clung to Juli.

How she knew what he intended baffled Moses, but he'd examine that later.

"I'm here," Moses said, stepping out of the shadows and toward the megaphone man. "Who are you?"

"I am nobody," the man replied. "But our commander, General Martin, will gladly accept your surrender."

Moses turned for one last look at his bride, only to realize the gang bangers from behind were now searching the entire group, piling weapons against one wall and people against another. Strong hands wrenched his arms behind his back and secured his wrists with a zip tie.

Such a simple design. A few cents of plastic molded into a line, with a catch-hold to secure the loose end in place. Practically indestructible, except with a sharp object, and cheaper than dirt. He'd carried the Army's version with him on patrol in the Middle East for years. He'd lost more zip ties than these bozos had combined.

And now, one bound his hands. It bothered him he didn't know the color.

His arms jerked upward, and a boot kicked his rear, pitching Moses forward onto his knees.

"You'll kneel before your superiors," the man growled into his ear as a pair of shined leather shoes entered his field of vision.

Moses fixed his eyes on the loose gravel, focusing his mind on the speckled gray rock instead of those shoes. The blows came fast. First to his lower back, then to his gut. Then his jaw. Moses reminded himself to let the punches move him. "Rolling with it" is what they called it.

He bounced around like a punching bag, his knees anchored to the loose blacktop, his upper body bobbing and weaving. Shuffling feet blended with the grunts of his assailants.

"No! Mose —" Juli's yell cut off.

He exhaled, waiting for the gunfire that would end his family. End those kids. None came. But the footsteps grew fainter until his own groans and the gang bangers' taunts were the only sounds.

Shiny Shoes grasped his shoulders, bringing Moses's gaze up to his.

Moses blinked at the man before him. Short stature, well-muscled, but lean with a hooked nose. His dark hair held only scant threads of gray sparkling in the moonlight. A trim mustache defined his upper lip, but the rest of his face was bare.

All that was normal for a Hispanic or an Italian, maybe a mixed-race man. Except his eyes. Those weren't normal. Like pools of ink, the man's black eyes swallowed the darkness.

Pure evil.

That's what Moses was looking at. Evil in the flesh.

"Who are you?" Moses choked out, aghast at his slip before his training caught up.

Shiny Shoes slapped him across the face with his bare hand, the imprint aching like none of the other punches had. Moses kept his mouth shut while working his jaw, even though he knew the man saw his discomfort.

"You'll call me Supreme Commander Martin. And I'm your new ruler." Martin stepped away. "Take him to my office and prep him."

So, he was to be tortured. No surprise there. He figured as much. Rough hands dragged Moses to his feet and shoved him headfirst into the back of a sleek black Tigr.

The low hum of the engine startled Moses. Shouldn't this vehicle be as noisy as their Army Humvees? Was it electric? If so, how did they charge it? And why? These were massive, inefficient. Definitely not suited for an electric battery. Unless this was a prototype of alternative fuel. Leave it to the Russians to pawn off their experiments on these scum.

Surrounded by hostiles with their mask-covered faces, Moses knew he'd be taking "roll with it" to a whole new level. If he survived the night, that was.

Chapter 11: Julianna

The tables had turned, and Juli didn't know what to think about her situation.

Taken prisoner. Being held in, of all places, her old high school gym. Sleeping in the chilly space on a threadbare cot. Eating cold oatmeal and peas from a can. No idea where her husband was.

After the gangs had separated Moses from the rest of their group, they'd beaten Moses. Ari dragged her away kicking and screaming, the enemy fighters laughing at her distress.

She'd waited up that first night, half expecting Moses to appear at her cot-side. And now her entire body ached and her limbs felt like lead pipes.

He wasn't coming. They'd taken him. Maybe even killed him. All for being a skilled military operator. For resisting their destruction and the rule of this Martin guy.

Looking at the hundreds sleeping roughly just like her, Juli thought she understood what Martin's aim was. Subjugate the masses and lock them behind walls. As

Martin's men had herded their small group of adults and teenagers into the Walnut Hills High School gym, she'd seen what would eventually be a massive concrete wall under construction on the other side of I-71.

Her skin crawled at being held prisoner inside her own city. Behind unscalable walls. Governed by a power-hungry drug lord. Would they make her traffic drugs? She'd rather die. Would she be a slave to these brutes? Again, she'd choose death over slavery. Every time.

But they'd stripped her weapons and anything else useful.

She sat up on her cot, dangling her legs over the edge.

"I'll be right back," Ari said, leaving Juli with her thoughts and the child who had curled herself against Ari, seeking warmth and reassurance amid the fear and uncertainty perfuming the gym.

The girl lifted bright blue eyes to Juli's, blinking back her tears until they fell unhindered onto the canvas cot. Juli wouldn't lie and reassure her. Wouldn't tell her that Mami and Papi would be here soon. It was best the child realized things would never be okay again. Though she worried what would happen to them once the gangs — forget that, army — finished the wall.

Soon, the girl's breathing evened out and her eyes closed. At least someone could sleep with the midday noise. Juli smiled gently at the girl and said a silent prayer.

Donna's approach grabbed her attention. They'd arrived at the high school about the same time, Ian's group having likewise been pursued, though most of that group, including Ian, had escaped. Donna, never the best runner, had trailed behind, allowing Martin's men to catch her so that others could get away. Ian and the rest hadn't appeared yet, giving Juli hope they'd made it out alive.

Donna sat next to her, weaving a hand through Juli's arm and clasping hands. Juli kept her face carefully blank at the paper pressed into her palm.

"Have you eaten yet today, *amiga*?" Donna's eyes held a sparkle at using Juli's native language, but Juli struggled to take comfort in her friend's effort. There was nothing to be joyful about in this place, and any trace of joy would alert suspicions.

"If you can call that gruel food, then yes. I've eaten." Juli rubbed her barely there baby bump with her free hand. "How?" she whispered, clutching the message.

"Matthew escaped capture, though Angie got left behind. And we have someone on the inside." Donna whispered back. "The gangs don't know the cipher somehow, despite the mole. They are going mad trying to decode it." She chuckled, then shifted and wrapped an arm around Juli's shoulders. "I'm sorry about Moses."

"Not your fault, unless you were the mole." The hard edge to Juli's voice surprised even her. Juli didn't hold on to grudges. There was no use in it. Usually. Today, however, anger consumed her, nearly blinding her with its intensity.

"Not me. Though I think I know who it was."

Juli felt Donna scribble a "T" onto her shoulder and exhaled loudly. Of course, the young man whose mother had a broken leg. She should've suspected something wasn't right when he'd refused freedom. Did his mother even exist? Why hadn't they checked out his story? Juli realized she hadn't seen Toby at the high school. How could she be so naïve?

There'd been so much going on. Juli had been worried about Moses, about herself becoming a single mother. And now, that's what she was, unless El Paco released Moses.

"But if he's the mole, why doesn't Martin know the cipher? He used it all the time," Juli asked.

Donna shrugged. "Maybe he changed his mind? Held something back? Got killed?"

"I hope we aren't meeting," Rev said as he passed in the row next to them.

"Nope," Juli said, standing and shoving her hands into her jeans pockets, burying the note with them. "I need to use the restroom."

Juli left Donna and navigated through the crowd, greeting those she knew and hugging the youngest, trying to reassure them that one day they'd have something more than oatmeal and canned peas to eat. She thought it funny that her role in life had hardly changed, despite nuclear bombs, an EMP and a civil war. She was still reassuring kids that someday life would be better.

The trouble was, did Juli still believe that herself?

She stepped into the women's locker room, shutting the stall door behind her. Crouching to examine every nook and cranny for surveillance cameras and finding none, Juli pulled the note out. She released her ponytail to let her curly hair shield the note as she sat on the toilet seat.

Made it outside the city. Send refugees to the place the brothers lived. - J

Juli wracked her brain. What brothers? She should know this, otherwise he would've given more details or a different clue. Juli tore the note into pieces and flushed them down the toilet. Leaving the stall, she stared at the mirror, not seeing her own face, as she washed her hands. Brothers. Outside the city. Someplace they lived.

Jed was heading north to Canada. But he had started in Indiana. Did that mean he was north in Indiana or had he crossed into Ohio? Ohio made more sense since Canada was a straight shot north across Lake Erie. That was a faster route — and safer — than navigating around Detroit or Chicago, or north through Michigan.

Juli turned the water off and dried her hands, hardly noticing the group of teenage girls enter the locker room, comforting one in tears. She nodded to them and walked the hallway, pacing back and forth until it hit her.

Jed and his people had gone to Dayton and had holed up at the Wright Brothers' historical home in downtown Dayton. She and Moses had visited before the nuclear attacks, feeding her obsession with all things aviation after attending the Dayton Air Show. The realization those beautiful planes would never touch the sky again saddened her. But now she knew where Jed was.

She returned to her cot, sitting down next to Donna.

"Figured it out, huh?" Donna smiled at her. "Took me a while, too. That came via Matthew. Sent another note in cipher. He's heading there with a group of fast runners. Said to look after Angie."

"This can't go any further than the two of us, maybe Rev."

"He already knows. Did you destroy it?"

Juli chuckled. "As fast as I could. Even before I figured it out."

"What now?"

Juli laid back, her legs extended into the aisle and her head hanging over the other edge. She lifted her hands into the stream of sunlight coming in through the nearby windows. "I guess we rest until they tell us where we'll live. And hope everyone survives. I don't think they'd bother feeding us unless they wanted to keep us alive. There's some bigger plan going on. If we knew, I think we'd weep."

Chapter 12: Moses

A fist cocked his jaw, sending him rolling to his right.

The pain centered him.

"Who are the other leaders?" the man growled in Moses's face as his spittle landed on Moses's cheek. His breath stunk of alcohol, probably something cheap.

Moses breathed in and out through his nose, his eyes focused on the wall.

Maybe Juli could get an apartment with another young mother. Perhaps even Angie and Matthew, if they hadn't tried to flee. Or she'd live around other intact families. Not that there were many of those.

The bastards kept referring to a "new normal." Moses swallowed back a snort of laughter. Who did they think they were anyway? A "new normal"? What the hell even was that?

At least they'd released the non-combatants and he didn't have to hear his bride's screams.

He rested his head against his upper arm, allowing the chains suspended from the ceiling to stretch his shoulders as he wiped the man's spittle from his cheek. A kick to the back spun him, making him lose his footing again. Moses clenched his fists around the cuffs and lifted himself to stand.

"We can do this for days."

So could he.

More punches in his unguarded, vulnerable belly. Then to his face and back as his attackers surrounded him.

They knew squat, and he wasn't about to enlighten them. These guys were a bunch of pansies compared to Ranger School.

The metal door to his prison cell swung open, clanging against the concrete wall behind it and rebounding into the man following Martin into the room.

"It's in your best interests to cooperate," Martin said, kicking a wooden chair that had seen better days to sit backward in it, his elbows resting on the back. Martin's black eyes pierced Moses's, steeling his resolve.

Examining him, Moses realized why that name "El Paco" had been so familiar. He was the same man as the drug lord known as "El General," now otherwise known as Supreme Commander Martin. The FBI wanted posters at the Dayton PD headquarters included a grainy surveillance photo of Martin. Drug trafficking, human trafficking, conspiracy, money laundering, murder, illegal sales of banned substances, gun-running. You name it, Martin had done it. That's why he'd used an alias for his alias.

Add to Martin's rap sheet overthrowing a democratic government and installing himself as dictator. The crowning jewel of Martin's accomplishments.

Martin smiled at Moses. A smile filled with the cunning and the cruelty of a spider made human. A smile that said, "you're caught in my web and I'm not letting you go until I get what I want."

Too bad Moses wasn't in the mood to give Martin what he wanted. He had one goal in this interrogation session. And it wasn't to survive.

"It's time." Martin stood, pressing his tanned hands down crisp dress pants, as if a wrinkle would dare threaten their perfection.

The guards who had beaten Moses without mercy walked out, dragging back in a hose and a rickety chair.

Moses's chains released from the ceiling, and he crumpled into a tight ball on the floor. Conserve energy. Keep your mouth shut. Ignore them. He'd work this plan until they left him alone or he had what he wanted. They didn't realize it, but Moses held all the cards in this poker game they played.

After tying him into the chair and tipping it backward, the men shoved a hose into his face. The water gushed out and up his nose. Moses allowed himself to sputter and cough, breathing only when they removed the hose. After he lost his lunch in the second round of waterboarding, Moses let his body react, the guards flinching away every time he hurled. During the entire session, Martin stood against one of the cell walls, a guard shielding him from Moses's vomit. Smug satisfaction filled Martin's black, soulless eyes. He looked like a caricature of a devil savoring human suffering from a bad B movie.

Moses spat the last of the nearly sewage water out of his mouth and wiped his face on his soaked shoulder.

"Not even a peep? We can do this all day."

Moses nodded curtly, dropping his head to his chest to empty his sinuses. His hands cuffed behind his back made this nearly impossible.

"They fled," Moses said in a whisper.

Martin exploded from the wall and shoved Moses's shoulders, toppling him backward. Moses curled inward as the chair splintered beneath him and Martin's men descended on him like wolves on a fresh kill.

Moses came awake gradually, not moving from his curled-up position on the floor. He heard several distinct breathing patterns and knew he wasn't alone. He wondered how long he'd been out, even as he took stock of his body.

Moses figured Martin would take the bait and had expected the assault. His exhaustion derailed his attempts to stay in the moment, though. He considered going back to sleep.

He blinked a few times to clear his vision and smiled at the guard inside his cell. He rolled onto his back and noted another, but no Martin. Seemed he had grown bored.

"Where is he?"

"You'll address your betters properly." The man's voice sounded like gravel rustling through dense jelly — a deep Texan drawl punctuated by growls and grunts. "That's Supreme Commander to you, scum. Now, where are the other leaders?"

"I told you they left the city days ago," Moses said, lifting his eyes to connect with the man's, conveying his sincerity. Moses doubted Martin would buy his lie, but he'd try anyway. "I can do this all day. Or I can tell you what I know, not what you want to know. Your choice."

The guard slapped Moses on his left temple, his ear ringing with the impact and his vision spinning. He shook his head like a dog and expelled air and mucus from his nose.

"Thanks for clearing out that sinus," Moses said, wiping his face on his sleeve.

He lifted his gaze, noting how the guard fidgeted. Shifting weight ever so slightly back and forth, giving away his nerves.

"I can tell you where Army munitions are. Lots of them."

They'd find them, eventually. Moses was positive about that. Maybe had already found them. But this was his one chip to play.

The guard's eyes widened, communicating his greed for more guns and ammo. He spun and left the room, gesturing to the other guard to stay.

"You should tell him everything you know. Save yourself. Or else you'll die after what Martin has planned."

Moses scoffed. He knew he was a dead man walking. And he didn't care one iota. He'd survived tours in the Middle East, gang warfare in the US, and weeks in an apocalyptic hell in his own city. Moses would live a day at a time and see who won.

The metal door banged open and Martin stomped in, followed closely by the guard who'd left.

"So, you're ready to talk, huh?"

Martin crossed his arms over his chest, a Cheshire cat smile filling his face. Moses had never seen an uglier mug in his life.

"I have demands."

Martin laughed. "Demands. Out with it, stubborn cuss."

"The woman named Juli stays alive. Whatever you're doing with survivors, she had nothing to do with my rebel groups. Plus, she's pregnant. You want to repopulate the nation, right?"

Martin was a statue. The only sign of his agreement was a twitch of the lips.

"Her safety for my information." Moses paused, staring into the black hole of Martin's eyes. His eyes hardly had any whites, unnerving Moses.

Martin nodded crisply, and the men flanking Moses shoved him to kneel before Martin.

"That's better." Martin smiled. The smile of a snake, lacking any joy or mirth. "Now the munitions. Your bitch is safe with me."

Moses clenched his jaw against lashing out at Martin. If the man even touched a hair on Juli's head, Moses would come after him. Dead or not.

"Get me a map of Ohio, Indiana, and Illinois. I'll mark locations where the Army stored all our supplies, including munitions. And they're not where you think. Sure, some are at National Guard facilities, but the number of nondescript warehouses under Army control will shock you."

Martin licked his lips. "Now, we're talking. This will be a wonderful collaboration."

Moses prayed his dead Army superiors would forgive his treason, but nothing was more important than Juli's safety. Nothing.

Chapter 13: Julianna

Juli's fingers curled into her hair, pulling a thick curl and twining it between her thumb and forefinger. She was only half aware of her fidgeting, focusing on the line of prisoners making their way past her new one-bedroom apartment on the fifth floor of the old condo complex at Sawyer Point Park.

The prisoners looked like a chain gang out of America's Civil War history or a parade of prisoners of war taken captive on some Pacific island. Thick cuffs around their necks connected each person in a chain to the one ahead and behind them. Zip ties secured their hands behind them, forcing them to march in unison or risk strangulation if they fell. Juli had never felt such disgust at what human beings did to each other.

She shook possible images of torture and deprivation from her mind. Of too-gaunt faces using dirty hands to scoop gruel into mouths, flies on lips and buzzing in hair. She told the sounds of barking hounds and the whimpers of abused prisoners to leave. Then she prayed her Moses was in that long line and not dead.

Anything except dead. Juli would figure out how to free her husband from whatever prison he ended up in. But how would she know where they took him? He had to survive until she figured it out. And she would.

Juli leaned her forehead against the glass, allowing the chill to seep into her soul. When Martin's fighters had taken Moses away, Juli felt like they'd taken her soul with them.

Light pressure on her shoulder startled her from her inspection.

"Juliana, please come away from the window," the woman said, her hand gently turning Juli into the one-bedroom apartment she inhabited with another family. Overall, it was more comfortable than the cot in the Walnut Hills gym. But she didn't know the couple and their teenaged daughters before being crammed together in the apartment.

"Malina, please," Juli said, returning to the window. "I need to see if he's alive."

"They are like ants down there." The woman's frown furrowed lines into her forehead. The teenagers carried on their argument over who had to collect the family's rations that day. "Girls. Stop arguing. You'll go together."

"Mama, you made me do it alone yesterday. It should be her turn."

Juli tuned out the bickering, her eyes hungry for any sign of Moses.

There. Just coming around the bend in the River Walk, where the path emerged from under the bridge.

Juli threw herself from the window and sprinted out of the apartment, the dark, empty hallway swallowing Malina's shouts to stay. Juli took the stairs two at a time, her feet pounding onto one landing after another. She clutched her side as an abdominal cramp set in. She wasn't far enough along yet to even feel her child move, but she slowed anyway.

With a yell, she launched into the lobby space, the guard on duty snapping his attention to her as she barreled onto the sidewalk.

"Wait, miss! You can't…"

The front door slammed shut behind her and she sprinted toward the river. Juli turned the corner into Sawyer Point Park and ran into a wall of flesh. Strong hands encircled her arms.

"Juli, don't," Rev said. "He wouldn't want you taken into custody."

The guard careened to a halt at her side, panting. "Good, you stopped." He walked back toward her building, resuming his post at the lobby door.

A crowd of onlookers had gathered a block away from the high-rise apartment building. Units which months earlier had rented for thousands of dollars a month now played host to the city's remaining occupants. A barricade and the park entrance separated them from the prisoners parading along the River Walk path.

Moses lifted his gaze to the crowd, his eyes flitting from one person to another until they landed on her.

His smile filled her body with warmth for the first time since Moses marched off into custody a week ago. Tears streamed down her cheeks, but Juli didn't dare pull her eyes from her husband. Moses smiled at her and mouthed, "I love you." He then nodded to Rev before his eyes drifted to her baby bump.

Their gazes remained locked together until the chains around his neck forced him to face forward, away from her, and he disappeared from view.

"Let's get back inside," Rev said as he tugged on Juli's arm.

She realized they were the last ones still gawking at the disappearing line of prisoners. There had been a few hundred men and women of mixed ethnicity and ages among the prisoners. Where were they being taken? Were they heading to the mass graves outside the city to join the dead in silent accusation of the new Martin regime?

"I have to find out where they're taking him."

"Not now, you don't." Rev wrapped an arm around her shoulders, and Juli shivered.

She was freezing cold again.

"Moses sacrificed himself. He gave them something, otherwise he'd be dead. And I bet he didn't give them what they wanted, seeing as you and I are still alive and kicking," Rev said.

Juli grunted. He had a point.

"So, we are going to lie low and play the long game. Let's not ruin his sacrifice by trying to go after him now."

Reverend Thompson nodded to the guard on duty at the park entrance, tapping her arm and gesturing with his chin for her to notice the enormous gun with Chinese markings on the barrel.

"Do you still want to run, little rabbit?" The smirking guard fingered the trigger, his nostrils flaring at her.

"No, sir. I'm not running."

Not yet, anyway. But someday, she would run. And Moses would be her destination.

Chapter 14: Julianna

Malina and her family walked ahead of Juli, heads bent as the guards escorting them up the hill and into Mt. Auburn paced alongside.

"Why can't we stay where we were?" Malina's older daughter asked.

"Shh," Malina whispered. "No questions, *mija*."

Juli agreed. She would have felt safer with Rev and Matthew's wife, Angie, nearby. But the government had resettled them elsewhere.

Being herded into a neighborhood of mostly burned-out homes didn't hold the greatest appeal.

The guards stopped abruptly at a tall barbed wire fence, calling to their colleagues on the other side to open the gate.

"How many more groups?" one asked.

The guard who'd threatened her the day before and called her "little rabbit" grunted his reply.

They were the last. Juli exhaled, wondering how many Hispanics would live in the area now named Little Havana. The guard in the lobby, the nice one who'd tried to stop her from running out, had told her they were being separated for their own good. That fights had broken out over scarce resources between Blacks, whites, Hispanics, and Asians.

But Juli knew better. They were separating everyone so that Martin could control them. It's what any dictator did. Separate people so they can't work together.

As they left downtown and started up the steep hill, Juli looked back at the Ohio River. Never again would she take for granted the little things in life, like being able to walk across a bridge or go shopping for a day.

She sped up, giving her legs their desire for speed, outpacing her former roommates. The constantly bickering teens made her head pound.

After passing a caved-in café and climbing Auburn Avenue, the guards assigned various families to different walk-ups along the street. Every other house had fire damage or was missing a roof, doors or windows.

The group had dwindled to just her and Malina's family when they reached the site of a premiere hospital in the city. Now, an enormous pit yawned at them, chain-linked fencing surrounding it and keeping her out. As she examined the charred remains of the once immaculate institution, her jaw fell open.

Did all of Cincinnati's major institutions look like this? She could still smell the stench of burned rubber and flesh, twisted metal rising skyward like soldiers at a tomb. Steeling herself, Juli breathed in and out through her nose and tried to keep her last meal from coming back up.

"Don't get too comfortable up here," the guard next to her said. He dipped his head. "I think you'll appreciate what our Supreme Commander has in store for your area. Soon you'll be returning downhill to a tree-lined village square and plenty of opportunities for jobs. Your child will have a beautiful new school and a *futbol* pitch."

She blinked up at him, wondering why he shared this.

The man gripped her arm and turned her toward a simple walkup across the street. Sheer stubbornness kept it standing upright. Wood pieces on the front lawn hinted at a former sign, while overgrown bushes told a story of long neglect, much longer than the recent troubles. Malina and her family disappeared into the first-floor entrance. The guard directed Juli toward the set of external stairs to the second-floor apartment.

Juli wondered how long this place would be home, how long she'd have to tolerate the noise of arguments from downstairs before being assigned someplace else. She also wondered who would labor to turn the rubble of the warehouses, stores, and homes into a habitable neighborhood. A shiver snaked through her at the realization that the people would. Not Martin's precious guards or soldiers or whatever they were.

Juli climbed the stairs, the guard yelling where she could pick up rations and her job assignment the next day before disappearing back down the hill. She wondered where Hispanic guards stayed and if she could avoid them altogether. Then she wondered when she'd see someone from another ethnicity, how long it would take Martin's plan to divide them physically to also divide them culturally.

Separated long enough, the various ethnic groups would develop their own culture, maybe even their own languages. At the very least, they'd regard each other with suspicion. If you didn't spend time with someone, preferably over a meal, how could you understand them?

Juli pushed open the door and entered the dusty space. Trash littered the floor, the stench making her run back outside to vomit over the railing. She wiped thin threads of spittle on her shirt and breathed in and out through her nose. She had no choice but to go back inside and clean out the apartment.

Closing her fingers over her nose, she sprinted inside, throwing open the windows not painted shut.

She dragged a weathered rocking chair out to the landing. Eyeing it and wondering how many splinters she'd later pull from her butt, Juli stood at the railing for now. Her hand settled onto her baby bump, while her gaze drifted south toward downtown and the setting sun to the west.

Ari waved at her from the front porch several houses away, joy infusing her hello. Several other young women joined Ari on the porch, raising hands to shade their eyes. Smiles of recognition lit their faces as Juli returned the wave. At least Ari wasn't alone.

Juli wondered how Angie fared. Juli figured Angie would find decent quarters in a Camp Washington high-rise with the rest of the Asian survivors. She prayed Angie would have help when she delivered her baby. Juli hoped Matthew had made it to Canada and could convince that government to oust Martin.

Of all the times to be pregnant, it had to be during the apocalypse. But Juli put her own pregnancy and impending delivery out of her mind. She would mourn her losses later.

With Rev and other Black survivors heading farther up the hill into Avondale, the Asians in Camp Washington at the bottom of the hill, and the whites relegated to Over-the-Rhine proper, Juli wondered how they'd keep any resistance alive.

The tunnels. Prohibition-era brewers and speak-easy operators, heck maybe even the mob, had originally dug the underground tunnels. Rough-hewn and unlit, they had lain hidden for decades until a boy discovered them a few years back.

Then Matthew had found an entire tunnel maze connecting Over-the-Rhine and Camp Washington. Tunnels with electric power and cement block walls. Tunnels they had only started to explore before every-thing went to hell. Matthew claimed they continued up the hill toward the university, but Juli had never ventured past their meeting space.

Could they use those tunnels to communicate? She sat in the rocking chair, despite the risk of splinters, and let the chair's creaking ground her. Juli would do anything to keep the resistance, and, by extension, Moses, alive. Even if everything moved, literally, underground.

Continue the journey with Moses and Juli in *Divided*.
Coming summer 2024.

Acknowledgements

While much of an author's work happens in isolation, I couldn't bring this novella to life without the help of many people.

First and foremost, to God, who birthed this story in my heart. To Steve who tolerated the awful early drafts and to Ruth, Zach and Katie Rose for being on this ten-year writing journey with me. Mom and Dad, thanks for believing in this crazy dream and for always opening my emails. It's seems small, but is like a shot of courage to me every month. Thanks also to Ps. Brian and my church community for their unwavering cheerleading.

Thank you to my writing community — to my editor, Amie, and cover designer Rebecca. It's a joy to work with such excellent professionals. To Raewyn, my virtual assistant — your wisdom with all things social media, newsletter and marketing has been invaluable. To my online writing friends at Women In Publishing and my real-life friends at Cincinnati Fiction Writers and my good friend Deb, thanks for being such awesome cheerleaders. To my Facebook Women Dystopian Authors group — y'all are the best. Thanks for the blurb sharpening skills, beta reading, and general encouragement. I wouldn't want to do this without y'all!

About the Author

CC Robinson has over two decades' experience in cross-cultural settings as a medical doctor working in post-civil war nations and as an associate pastor at a multi-ethnic congregation led by an African-American man in Cincinnati, the setting for *Upheaval* and the main dystopian series *Divided*. When she's not destroying and saving fictional worlds or torturing her characters, CC loves hiking, swimming, gardening, or just hanging out with her husband, three Gen Z kids, dog and cat in Cincinnati. Come find her on all the socials as *@ccrobinsonauthor* and say hi.

Find out more and sign up for her monthly newsletter at her website *ccrobinsonauthor.com*